上班

擴大詞彙、增進口說能力、加強翻譯，
實用會展英語一網打盡！

天天說英語

輕鬆駕馭國際會議

會展
規劃

商業
談判

展場
預定

U0075328

展覽
開幕

吳雲 主編

剛出社會的菜鳥不想讓公司丟臉？
初出茅廬的新鮮人想讓老闆看得上眼？
談判現場想要在外國廠商面前有好表現？

千萬別因為英語能力差而讓自己職業生涯受限！

口說翻譯，ready to speak ！

CONTENTS

目錄

Chapter 3
Event Planning and Budgeting 會展策劃與預算

CONTENTS

Chapter 6
Negotiating on Exhibiting Space 展位談判

Section 1
Interpretation Activities

Section 2
Speaking Activities

Chapter 7
Hiring A Stand 申請展位

Section 1
Interpretation Activities

CONTENTS

Chapter 8
Personal Sales Calls 銷售拜訪（電話）

Chapter 9
Hiring People and Loaning Properties 租借物品 / 租用人員

Chapter 10
Safety and Security Service 安保服務

CONTENTS

Chapter13
Attending the Event 參加展會

CONTENTS

Chapter 1
Enquiring about Holding a Conference 會議諮詢

Go over and expressions the following words.

fund raising gala			募捐晚會
rehearsal		n.	排演
Murphy's law			莫非定律
set aside			留出
so what			那又怎麼樣
sponsor		n.	贊助者
financial outlay			經濟支出
preliminary		adj.	初期的，開始的
clearly defined responsibility			明確的職責劃分
indispensable		adj.	不可缺少的

Section 1
Interpretation Activities

A. Sentence Interpretation

1. First, find out the equivalents of the following words.

1. retailer	
2. recreation facilities	
3. 獎勵旅遊	
4. 同義詞	
5. 區分	
6. 簡要介紹一下	

7. 無過多要求	

2. Read the following material to your partner; ask him or her to put them into Chinese or English.

1. Comparing both conventions, the biggest difference is size.

2. What's more, they look for attractive locations, recreation facilities, choice of restaurants, etc.

3. It was E. F. MacDonald who innovated the idea of Incentive travel.

4. One big advantage of exhibiting at this show is that we can meet retailers form all over the country.

5. By this design, you can easily find the show you want to visit.

6. 怎麼區分「seminars」和「conventions」呢？你認為它們是同義詞嗎？

7. 你說的不夠完整「congress」在歐洲普遍使用，並用於國際會議。

8. 首先，讓我向你們簡要介紹一下我們中心。

9. 在諸多獎勵形式中，為何偏偏選擇旅遊這種獎勵形式？

10. 我意思是說他們對會議設施並無過多要求。

B. Passage Interpretation

1. First, find out the equivalents of the following words.

1. overlap		5. 消費者展覽	
2. quantify		6. 分離出	

| 3. premise | | 7 賺取利潤 | |
| 4. 貿易展覽 | | 8 同時進行 | |

2. Read the following passages and translate them into Chinese or English.

Passage 1

Meetings, whether they are conferences or conventions, Increasingly overlap with Incentive travel. This is because companies both at home and abroad are attaching much importance to rewarding Good performance of employees.

Association meetings are staged where local associations are highly active. Many international associations, like the World Exposition Organization, choose a venue for practical reasons, Including the supporting interests.

While the meeting industry is concerned with communicating information, it is hard to quantify the different types of meetings involved. What makes up a meeting depend on the minimum number of attendees, the length of time, the subjects or activities and sometimes the type of premises.

Your Answer

_____

_____

_____

_____

_____

_____

_____

_____

_____

Passage 2

　　和協會會議相同，展覽亦需要周密的計畫和組織，這主要是因為展覽的籌備期較長、初期風險較大。一旦貿易展覽和消費者展覽成功開展，總是趨向成為定期展覽，規模不斷壯大，從而分離出更多的專業展覽會。

　　展商可能有自己單獨的展臺，或者聯合成為一個團體，他們時常提前預訂展位，以保證得到最好的位置。

　　與會議相比較而言，創辦成功的展覽通常能夠為供應商和展覽會主辦方贏取利潤。展覽和會議時常同時進行；大型的或者專業貿易展覽會一般在展覽期間穿插一些作為增加吸引力或發布資訊的研討會，參展者可選擇性地參與其中。

Your Answer

_____

_____

_____

_____

_____

_____

_____

_____

_____

Reference Answers

A. Sentence Interpretation

1. words

1. retailer	零售商
2. recreation facilities	娛樂設施
3. 獎勵旅遊	Incentive travel/tour
4. 同義詞	synonym
5. 區分	distinguish
6. 簡要介紹一下	give a sketch of
7. 無過多要求	less demanding

2 .sentences

1. 比較起來，兩個會議的最大區別在於會議規模不相同。

2. 再者，他們需要的是迷人的景點、娛樂設施、精選餐廳等。

3. 正是 E. F. MacDonald 創立了獎勵旅遊的概念。

4. 參加這個展覽的一大優點在於能接觸到來自全國各地的零售商。

5. 這種設計的優點在於幫助你迅速找到你要參觀的展覽。

6. How do you distinguish seminars from conventions? Do you think they are synonyms?

7. And to complete your list, congress is most commonly used in Europe and in international events.

8. To start with, let me give you a brief sketch of our center.

9. Among all forms of rewards, why are people given Incentive travels?

10. What I mean is that they are less demanding for meeting facilities.

B. Passage Interpretation

1. word

1. overlap 重疊	2. quantify 用數量表示
3. premise 房屋連地基	4. 貿易展覽 trade fair
5. 消費者展覽 consumer fair	6. 分離出 to hive off
7. 贏取利潤 to generate profits	8. 同時進行 to be held in parallel

2. paragraph

▌**Passage 1**

　　會議，無論他們是一般會議或大會，正漸漸與獎勵旅遊相重合。這是國內外公司都重視對職員的良好表現進行獎勵的結果。

　　協會會議總是在地方性的協會高度活躍的地方召開。許多國際協會，如世博會，出於實際原因選擇舉辦地點，包括當地民眾的支持力度。

　　會議用於傳遞資訊時，很難說有多少種不同種類的會議。構成會議的要素取決於出席者最少人數，會期的長短，主題或活動類型，以及所選會址類型。

▌Passage 2

Like association meetings, exhibitions need careful planning and organization, involving long lead times and initially a high degree of risk. Once established, trade fairs and consumer exhibitions tend to continue to be held as a regular calendar event, invariably growing in size and hiving off more specialist exhibitions.

Individual exhibitors may occupy stands exclusively or join together as an associated group in a larger assembly, and often need to reserve space well ahead to secure prime positions.

Compared with meetings, established exhibitions usually generate operating profits both for the hall providers and organizers of the events. Exhibits and meetings are often held in parallel; large or specialized trade fairs commonly Include optional seminars as an additional attraction and related source of information.

Section 2
Speaking Activities

A. Specialized Terms

Match the expressions on the left with the best equivalent Chinese on the right.

1. event   A. 職業會議策劃者

2. sponsor   B. 會議中心

3. planner   C. 與會者

4. attendee   D. 主旨發言人

5. venue   E. 大型活動（會展、節慶等）

6. convention center   F. 目的地管理公司

7. keynoter   G. 贊助方

8. CVB (Convention and Visitors H. 會議觀光局
Bureau)

9. CMP (Certified Meeting Plan- I. 會後旅遊
ner)

10. DMC (Destination Manage- J. 註冊會議策劃師
ment Company)

11. PCO (Professional Conference K. 會議策劃者
Organizer)

12. post-conference tour　　　　L. 會展場地

B. Sample Conversation

read aloud.

Situation: A foreign planner calls the sales office of Taipei Convention and Visitors Bureau. He asks various questions about holding an annual association conference in the city. The clerk at the reception desk is answering him by providing the information the caller enquires about.

（一位國外會議策劃者打電話到臺北市會議觀光局。他問了許多關於在該市舉辦年度協會的問題。一位接待員在電話裡一一作答。）

Clerk: Taipei Convention and Visitors Bureau. May I help you?

Planner: Yes. I'm John Stevens, calling from New Orleans. We're planning to hold a conference in your city. So I was wondering if you could give me some relevant information.

Clerk: It's a pleasure. What would you like to start with?

Planner: Would you tell me if we could hold the conference at a hotel or at a convention center of the city?

Clerk: It all depends. For how Many attendees?

Planner: About 60 people.

Clerk: Then I think a medium-sized meeting room will do. All hotels in the city each have conference centers offering such meeting rooms.

Planner: Good. One more thing, what will the weather be like there in October?

Clerk: In Taipei, October is the most agreeable of the season, with clear sky casting golden sunshine, and gentle breeze blowing. The temperature is about 18—23 ℃, or 64.4—73.4 ℉.

Planner: Sounds wonderful. We plan to have a post-conference tour, and it seems we've chosen the right time. By the way, what can we expect to see there?

Clerk: There are a Good variety of places worth sightseeing both in the city proper and the neighboring towns. For a shopping tour, you may go to Breeze Center. For a commanding view over the whole city, you may mount on to the Taipei 101.

Planner: You can certainly help us a lot with the tour, will you?

Clerk: Sure, we can. We can also help you liaise a property to hold your conference once you've make a decision.

Planner: Thank you very much for the information. We'll let you know our decision in a week's time.

Clerk: Please feel free to contact us if you have any question in your mind.

Planner: We will. Thanks again. Goodbye.

Clerk: Goodbye. Thanks for calling.

C. Functional Expressions

Read aloud and practice with your partner.

1. How to elicit questions politely	Response
Can I help you?	Yes, I'd like to be told some general information about the city's meeting facilities.
May I help you?	Yes, we're planning a meeting.
How may I help you?	I want to know the dress code for attending the conference.
How may I assist you?	It's Su-Hui calling from China and we plan to hold a conference in UK.

2. How to make inquiries politely	Response
Excuses me, would you mind answering a few questions?	No, not at all.
Excuses me, I wonder if you'd mind answering a few questions?	Of course not.
Could you tell me what the weather is like there?	Yes, certainly.
Do you think you could tell me what the weather is like there?	Ok, I'll try.

I was wondering if you could tell me how to contact you?	You can either call us at 021-123456 or email us at cvb2010@hotmail.com.
May I ask how to contact you?	You can send us a fax to book the meeting.

3. How to verify information

Let me check. You said October. Is that right?

You did say 200 attendees, didn't you?

Forbes Global CEO Conference? Was it held in your place?

D. Role-play

Practise the conversations according to the situations.

● **Situation 1**

A major U.S. ABC Computer Corporation is calling the Taipei Claude Hotel to get some information about the group prices of rooms and seasonal prices of rooms. In pairs, try the Dialogue using your real names. One person will be the assistant manager for ABC Computer Corporation. The other person will be the sales manager for the Taipei Claude Hotel.

● **Situation 2**

You are a convention planner of Millipore Taipei Office. You would like to get some information about holding a conference in

Thompson Conference Center. You are calling Susan Zhu, sales clerk of Thompson Conference Center.

Information about you:

You are Joanna, a convention planner of Millipore Taipei Office.

Intention: Hold a three-day annual sales meeting

Place: Thompson Conference Center

Time: Feb.14th ——Feb.16th, 2005

Number of attendees: 27

Room reservation:

3 presidential suites and 12 standard rooms for 3 nights

3 meeting rooms (1 for 10 people, 1 for 8 and the other for 9 on Feb. 15th and 16th

Activities during the meeting:

Holding an annual dinner on the night of Feb.14th, requirements:

A small dinning room with 3 tables

A toastmaster capable of both Chinese and English

The name lists on each table

Meeting room facilities:

1 overhead, 1 slide projectors and screen, booth draping tables, 1 podium, overhead projector pen

Questions the clerk might ask you:

1. What types of hotel rooms are available in your Center?

2. What types of meeting rooms are available in your Center?

3. What types of meeting equipment do you offer in your Center?

4. What tourist attractions will we expect to sightsee?

● **Situation 3**

You are Mary Zhu, a clerk of Convention Office. You are answering a phone call from a convention attendee who would like to get some information about it. Use the information below to answer the questions from the prospect.

Your card:

Information about you:

Room reservation:

Hilton Hotel with a room rate of $100 per day

Mandarin Oriental Hotel with a room rate of $120 per day

Jinjiang Hotel is nearer to the convention center.

Temperature: 18-23 °C

Activities of post-conference tour:

- Sightseeing both in the city proper and the neighboring towns
- Shopping
- Mounting on to the Taipei 101
- Sun Yat-Sen Memorial Hall, etc.

Information you need to get from the other party:

Name of the caller?
Name of Convention?
Intention?
Room reservation?
Date?

The prospect's card:

Information about the prospect:

Shirley White: an attendee of the convention from U.S.
Convention: the 22nd World Nursing Congress, from May 24th to 28th
Intention: make sure the arrangement of the convention
Room reservation: Hilton Hotel with a room rate of $100 per day
Mandarin Oriental Hotel with a room rate of $120 per day
Date: from May 23rd to 28th

Questions the prospect might ask:

Wish to make sure of the arrangements of the congress?
Wish to reserve a room?
Climate of the city?
Temperature:Fahrenheit(F=Cx1.8+32;C=F=(F-32)/1.8)
Activities of post-conference tour?

Reference Answers

A. Specialized Terms

1.E   2.G   3.K   4.C   5.L   6.B   7.D   8.H
9.J   10.F   11.A   12. I

Chapter 2

Booking an Event 招展商會展預訂

Learn and expressions these words.

top sales performance			傑出銷售業績
justify		v.	證明
client appreciation event			客戶聯誼活動
pique		v.	刺激
sales executive			銷售主管人員
initiative		n.	主動行動
motivation		n.	刺激
entail		v.	需要
contagious		adj.	觸染性的
prospect		n.	可能性很大的潛在客戶
encounter		v.	遇見
convincingly		adv.	使人信服地
crane		n.	起重機
return on investment			投資回報
enterprise		n.	企業
conference delegate			會議代表

Section 1
Interpretation Activities

A. Sentence Interpretation

1. First, find out the equivalents of the following words.

1. innovation		6. 經裝修一新	
2. attendance		7. 影像設備	
3. distraction		8. 省去 …… 的麻煩	
4. keynoter		9. 滿足要求	
5. attendee		10. 會議套餐	

2. Read the following to your partner for him or her to put them down in Chinese or English.

1. I've heard so much about what your firm has been doing in the area of printer technology and application. And I'm eager to hear more about your innovation.

2. What is your average attendance at your annual convention?

3. Our meeting rooms are free from distraction so that the keynoters can make his/her speeches well understood.

4. The speaker is able to control lights, sound and projection from a single station because each meeting room has built-in audio and visual aids with individual control stations in each possible subdivision of the space.

5. Your center may not be as attractive to our attendees as the new resort in your area.

6. 我了解到你認為我們的中心不夠現代化。但是，我們的客房和會議室已經裝修一新，擁有全套在本地區頗具競爭力的設施。

7. 我們這裡的視聽設備將大大地提升你們的培訓會議，難道您不這樣認為嗎？

8. 我們提供 24 小時會議室服務，這樣就能夠省去每天會議結束後搬運培訓材料的麻煩，同時也無需在第二天重新安裝設備。

9. 我認為我們的專案能夠滿足你們的要求。我們找個時間一起吃頓午飯並討論一下貴方的培訓會議，您意下如何？

10. 有關我們的中心和我們近期為本地企業設計的會議套餐，我想您一定會感興趣的。

B. Passage Interpretation

1. First, find out the equivalents of the following words.

1. double occupancy		6. 抵達	
2. brochure		7. 離店	
3. fact sheet		8. 提前報到者	
4. accolade		9. 出行安排	
5. 無需說		10. 住宿服務	

2. Read the following passages to yourself and render them into Chinese or English.

Passage 1

We have already established our convention rates for this year. Currently, our Group Plan No.1 during August are 3,500 NT dollars single and 3,750 NT dollars double occupancy. Group Plan No. 2 Includes room, breakfast/lunch/dinner and is currently 6,000NT dollars single and 7,000 NT dollars double occupancy.

I've enclosed several descriptive brochures along with a most comprehensive fact sheet. As you can see, we do make available this area's most complete convention hotel. We are the only hotel in our area that has its own 18-hole championship course and a tennis center. Also, please keep in mind that we are a five-star hotel. We've maintained this accolade for the past 10 years.

Your Answer

_____

_____

_____

_____

_____

_____

_____

_____

Passage 2

　　週二我們通過電話，談得非常愉快。無需說，我們很高興能有機會在八月份為貴協會服務。我們將在以下時間為你們提供十分舒適的的住宿服務：抵達時間—8 月 18 日，離開時間—8 月 22 日。我們能夠接待 8 月 17 日（星期二）的提前報到者，人數限於 30 以下。如果你可以接受我在這裡列出的安排，請書面告知。我將為您初步預留一些會議室，這樣，會議室就不會被租借給其他會議主辦方。再次向您表示感謝。請告知您的出行安排，以便我能留出時間陪同您參觀我們肯勞得會議中心。

Your Answer

_____

_____

_____

_____

_____

_____

_____

_____

Reference Answers

A. Sentence Interpretation

1. words

1. innovation	創新
2. attendance	參加會議的人數

3. distraction	干擾物
4. keynoter	主要發言人
5. attendee	與會者
6. 經裝修一新	completely renovated
7. 視聽設備	audiovisual equipment
8. 省去 ...... 的麻煩	Save the trouble
9. 滿足要求	Meet one's demand
10. 會議套餐	Meeting package

2. sentences

1. 對於貴公司在印表機技術和應用領域的長期努力，我知之甚多。我非常想了解更多的有關你們的創新故事。

2. 你們參加年會的人數平均是多少？

3. 我們的會議室沒有干擾物（噪音），主要發言人的講話能夠聽得很清楚。

4. 發言人在同一個地方就可以控制燈光、聲音和投影儀，這是因為每個會議室都有內置的聲像輔助設備，並且各自都有相對獨立的控制臺。

5. 比起你們的新度假勝地，貴中心對我們的與會者並不具有同樣的吸引力。

6. I learn that you don't feel our center is modern enough. But our rooms and meeting space have been completely renovated and offer all competitive amenities found in our area.

7. Don't you think our audiovisual equipment will greatly enhance your training sessions?

8. We offer 24-hour meeting room service, so that it can eliminate the trouble of removing training materials each evening and resetting equipment the next morning.

9. I think our program can best meet your demand. When could we meet for lunch to discuss your training sessions?

10. I though you'd be interested in hearing about our center and the meeting package we have just designed for local businesses.

B. Passage Interpretation

1. words

1. double occupancy	入住雙人房
2. brochure	小冊子
3. fact sheet	情況說明
4. accolade	榮譽
5. 無需說	needless to say
6. 抵達	arrival
7. 離店	departure
8. 提前報到者	early arrival
9. 出行安排	travel arrangement
10. 住宿服務	accommodation service

2. paragraph

▌**Passage 1**

　　我們已經制定了今年的會議價格。目前，八月份的一號團隊價格分別為單人房每夜間新臺幣 3,500 元，雙人房每夜間新臺幣 3,750 元。二號團隊價格為單人房每夜間新臺幣 6,000 元，雙人房每夜間新臺幣 7,000 元，包括客房、早餐 / 午餐 / 晚餐。 隨信附寄幾份介紹小冊子以及一份詳細的情況說明書。正如您所見，我們是本地設施齊全的飯店。當地只有我們這家飯店有 18 洞冠軍賽高爾夫球場和一個網球場。同時，請您記住我們是一家五星級飯店，我們保持著這項殊榮已有十餘載。

▌Passage 2

Certainly enjoyed our telephone conversation on Tuesday, and needless to say, we are gratified at the prospect of serving your association in August. We could very comfortably accommodate you for arrival Wednesday, August 18 with departure Sunday, August 22. We could accept some early arrivals on Tuesday, August 17. However, it would be limited to 30 guest rooms. If the arrangements I outlined are agreeable, please drop me a note and I will protect some meeting space for you on a tentative basis so that the space does not disappear to another meeting planner. Thank you again, and please let me know about your travel arrangements so that I can set aide the necessary time to personally acquaint you with the Claude.

Section 2
Speaking Activities

A. Specialized Terms

Match the expressions on the left with the best Chinese equivalent on the right.

1. MICE (meeting, Incentive tour, conference, exhibition)	A. 專家討論會
2. convention	B. 專業會議
3. conference	C. 產品發布會
4. plenary session	D. 會展（總稱）
5. seminar	E. 流程實習
6. workshop	F. 董事會議，全體成員會議
7. product launch;	G. 協會年會
8. board meeting	H. 研討會
9. fund-raiser	I. 募捐會
10. forum	J. 論壇
11. panel	K. 培訓會議
12. training session	L. 全體會議

B. Sample Conversation

read aloud.

Situation: Jiang Lin, director of convention sales department of Claude Convention Center, is meeting Mr. Rachel, the meeting planner, to discuss holding a meeting at the property.

肯勞得會議中心銷售部主任江林，他正在和會議主辦方 Rachel 先生就在該中心舉辦一次會議進行商談。

Director: Glad to meet you, Mr. Rachel. I'm Jiang Lin, director of convention sales department.

Mr.Rache: The pleasure is mine. I'm here to discuss with you about holding a meeting at your property.

Director: Happy to be of any help to you. What meeting is it?

Mr.Rache: An annual convention of the Translators Association. The attendees are top translators across the world.

Director: Can I see the name list of the attendees?

Mr.Rache: Certainly. Here it is.

Director: Oh, I see. There are 100 attendees. I think our medium-sized meeting room can serve the purpose.

Mr.Rache: Do you have sufficient number of breakout rooms? We have several seminars after the plenary session.

Director: At this time of high season, we'll use public space if necessary. Here are the convention brochures showing the details about meeting facilities.

Mr.Rache: Thank you. I shall consult with the president of the association. We'll let you know by fax once we've decided.

Director: Thank you for coming. We look forward to seeing you soon again.

C. Functional Expressions

Read aloud and practice with your partner.
Introducing the capacity and capability of the convention center

> Here is the rental rate list for equipment and personnel for the convention.
> We have some brand new imported equipment.
> It accommodates about 400 people.
> Our conference hall is multi-purpose.
> We have a fully-equipped convention center that provides complete secretarial service.
> We have all the state-of-art audiovisual equipment.

Giving further information about meeting booking

> You can hire our nightclub for private use.
> I will send you a support facilities list with a price list by fax.
> So you'd like to reserve our conference room for 3 days together with an overhead projector.
> I'll order a complete range of pens in different colors.

D. Speaking Up

Render the following into English by using as many language skills learnt as possible.

1. 這個多功能廳中心是主會議禮堂，能容納 400 人。
2. 這是我們的會議服務指南，裡面有關於會前、會中和會後服務的詳盡描述。

3. 能有這個機會為你們服務，我們感到十分榮幸。今天，我們能否從確定會議日期談起呢？

4. 該設備視聽品質俱佳。

5. 除免費房間外，會議工作人員還可以享用優惠價格房。

E. Role-play

Practise the conversations acoording to the situations.

Situation 1

You are a clerk with the local convention and visitors bureau (CVB). You are talking with a prospective customer on the phone, to arrange a fam trip to Xinyi, Taipei. You explain the tour schedule to the caller.

You should say or explain:

The duration of the fam. Tour.

What is Included (meals, transportation, etc.) and how are they arranged.

Whom the invitation Includes (spouse, other members of the selection committee, etc.).

The tour program: a. A camping to one of the best local destinations; b. Experience in the hotels, museums, restaurants and places of scenery and interes.

You are the Auto Expo project manager of the Galaxy Exhibition Company. You are planning an exhibition. You are visiting Mr. Li Ming with the local exhibition center. You discuss /negotiate the price terms for reserving exhibition space with Mr. Li Ming.

You should ask these questions:

Capacity of the center?
Price scale?
Counter offer?
Lower price?
Discount?
Wish to extend the closing hour of the day?

Reference Answers

A. Specialized Terms

1.E　　2.D　　3.G　　4.L　　5.H　　6.B　　7.C　　8.F
9.I　　10.J　　11.A　　12.K

D. Speaking Up

1. The center of the multi-purpose hall is the main conference auditorium seating 400.

2. This is our meeting prospectus, containing a complete description about services before, during and after meetings.

3. It's an honor to have this opportunity of serving your. Today, shall talk about the date of meeting, to begin with?

4. The equipment is of Good quality of both picture and sound.

5. Meeting staff can be offered rooms with a discounted room rate as well as complimentary rooms.

Chapter 3
Event Planning and Budgeting 會展策劃與預算

Go over and expressions the following words.

1 negotiation		n.	商議，談判
2 refund		n.	退款
3 package		n.	由好幾項內容構成的建議
4 preposition		n.	預先定位或放置
5 brand awareness			品牌認知度

Section 1
Interpretation Activities

A. Sentence Interpretation

1. First, find out the equivalents of the following words.

1 stay within the budget		6 一般管理費用	
2 loss leader		7 固定費用	
3 admission fee		8 可變費用	
4 profit-oriented event		9 收支平衡	
5 draft budget		10 淨利潤	

2. Read the following to your partner for him or her to put them down in Chinese or English.

1. The best financial history is that which occurs over a three-year period. In some cases it is not possible to construct a precise history and the event manager must rely upon what is

known at the time the budget is prepared or on estimates.

2. Once you have prepared a draft budget, seek the counsel of the accountant to review your budget and help you with establishing the various line items and account codes.

3. Producing a fair net profit is both challenging and possible for event management business. The challenge is that event managers must work with a wide range of clients and it is difficult to budget for each event carefully to ensure a net profit.

4. Since the invention of the spreadsheet program for computers, accounting has never been the same. Commercial software package such as Quicken have allowed small business people to record their journal entries quickly, accurately, and cost-effectively.

5. 會展活動的固定間接費用是指可預測的費用項目。例如：租金、薪水、保險費、電話費，以及支援活動管理正常運轉所需要的其他費用。

6. 一次會展活動，其固定費用的多寡並不取決於參加者人數的多少。比方說，租金就是一項固定費用。無論參加者人數是增加還是稍有減少，租金費用一般不會有什麼變動。

7. 可變費用的預測更加困難，原因是這些用品經常到最後時刻才購入，而且價格的波動較大。由於客戶經常到最後一分鐘才註冊，而且在許多會展活動中有越來越多的參加者臨時報名，因此，等到最後時刻才訂購用品是一件較為棘手的事情。

8. 創造可觀的利潤是會展經理的天然職責。淨利潤和毛利潤之間的差額，就是我們為舉辦會展活動而提供的固定間接費用資料。

B. Passage Interpretation

1. First, find out the equivalents of the following words.

budget preparatin	
estimate	
assumption	
邏輯思維方式	
捲入法律糾紛	

2. Read the following passages to yourself and render them into Chinese or English.

Passage 1

　　The budget represents an action plan that each successful event manager must carefully develop. Budget preparation is probably the most challenging part in financial management since the entire preparation is usually based on limited information or assumptions. To complete the budget preparation, you should come up with estimates based on assumptions.

Your Answer

_____
_____
_____
_____
_____
_____
_____
_____

Passage 2

　　據說活動管理者是用右腦思考的，常常會忽視重要的邏輯思維方式，而這種思維方式有助於確保活動能夠長期成功。忽視財務問題很容易破壞一個有創意、成功的活動，並損害管理者的聲譽，捲入法律糾紛。

Your Answer

_____
_____
_____
_____
_____
_____

Reference Answers

A. Sentence Interpretation

1. words

1 stay within the budget	控制預算
2 loss leader	虧本求購商品
3 admission fee	入會費
4 profit-oriented event	利潤導向型活動
5 draft budget	預算草案
6 一般管理費用	overhead expense
7 固定費用	fixed expense
8 可變費用	variable expense
9 收支平衡	break even
10 淨利潤	net profit

2. sentences

1. 財務歷史最好以三年的財務狀況為一個期限。如果出現無法準確建構一個財務歷史的情況時，會展經理人只有依靠在編制預算或進行預測時所掌握的情況編制預算。

2. 預算草案編制好之後，應當請會計師提出對預算編制的意見並說明設置各種明細科目和制定會計編號。

3. 對於會展管理公司而言，創造可觀的淨利潤既是一種挑戰，也是一種可能。所謂挑戰指的是，由於會展經理人接待的客戶範圍很廣，因此很難做到為所有的會展活動都編制出保證創造利潤的預算方案。

4. 在電腦試算表程式發明的助益下，會計職業的面貌已經煥然一新。像 Quicken 這樣的商務軟體包可以使小型企業快速、準確和經濟地註冊自己的日記帳。

5. Fixed overhead expenses of an organization are those predictable items such as rent, salaries, insurance, telephone, and other standard operating expenses required to support the event management business.

6. Fixed expenses of an individual event do not depend on the number of participants. For example, rent is a fixed expense. Rent expense usually does not vary when the number of participants Increases or decreases slightly.

7. Variable expenses are more difficult to predict because often they are purchased last minute from vendors and the prices may fluctuate. Due to last minute registrations and an Increase in walkup guests for a variety of events, it is extremely difficult to wait until the last minute to order certain items.

8. Event managers endeavor to produce a fair net profit. The difference between net profit and gross profit is the percentage of fixed overhead expenses that was dedicated to producing a specific event.

B. Passage Interpretation

1. words

budget preparatin	編制預算
estimate	估算

assumption	假設
邏輯思維方式	logical thinking abilities
捲入法律糾紛	produce legal implications

2. paragraph

▋Passage 1

　　預算是每一個成功的活動管理者都必須仔細制訂的行動計畫。由於預算制訂的整個過程都是建立在有限資訊和假設的基礎上，因此，它也許是財務管理工作中最具有挑戰性的部分。為完成預算的制訂工作，你應該在假設的基礎上作出一些預測。

▋Passage 2

　　It is said that event managers depend on the right side of the brain and often ignore the important logical thinking abilities that help ensure long-term success. Financial ignorance can easily wreck a creative, successful event management business and destroy one's reputation as well as produce serious legal implications.

Section 2
Speaking Activities

A. Specialized Terms

Match the expressions on the left with the best Chinese equivalent on the right.

1. payment schedule	A. 可歸還的
2. balance	B. 現金記帳法
3. full amount	C. 支付期限
4. unit price	D. 單價
5. deposit for calls	E. 桌面展示
6. refundable	F. 展臺展示
7. table top exhibit	G. 足額
8. area exhibit	H. 電話押金
9. booth exhibit	I. 可供預訂的展臺類型
10. options	J. 大型器材地面展示
11. exhibit assignments	K. 餘額
12. cash accounting	L. 展位分配

B. Sample Conversation

read aloud.

Situation: Mr. Ding are talking about planning Taiwan Toy Expositin with Mrs. Li.

Woman: Good morning, Mr. Ding. Nice to see you again.

Man: Good morning. Mrs. Li. Glad to meet you again too. I've come here to talk with you some details about Taiwan Toy Exposition.

Woman: It's a pleasure. What would you like to start with?

Man: Well, I think it's our wish that Taiwan Toy Exposition will be an international expo and attract toy manufacturers both at home and from abroad.

Woman: How many exhibitors are you expecting to attend this expo?

Man: We are expecting 200 leading foreign companies and 400 major domestic companies.

Woman: In that case, a large exhibition center is necessary.

Man: Sure. One more thing, we don't want to hold it in September. You know, another two toy exhibitions will be staged in Taichung and Kaohsiung at that time.

Clerk: I quite agree with you. There should be an interval of 3-6 moths between similar exhibitions. We prefer April, 2007.

Planner: It seems to be a Good time.

Clerk: By the way, what is your budget for the expo? Have you set aside some money for marketing?

Planner: Actually, we haven't finished budget preparation. To some degree, we want to make a decision after you have completed the draft expo plan. In terms of budget for marketing, we will take it into consideration.

Clerk: Yes, we are sure to complete the plan as soon as possible.

Planner: Thank you very much. It seems we have covered major points today?

Clerk: Yes, and thank you again for choosing our company as the expo organizer.

Planner: Not at all, we really trust you. Goodbye.

Clerk: Goodbye.

C. Functional Expressions

Read aloud and practice with your partner.

Discussing plans	Response
What are your plans for exhibitions next year?	We are planning 2 international expos.
What do you have in your mind to plan an exhibition?	I have no idea.
Do you know what it signifies?	It does show the unique character of Kaohsiung.
I think there should be an interval of 3-6 months between two similar exhibitions.	I cannot agree with you more.

D. Speaking Up

Render the following into English by using as many language skills learnt as possible.

1. 這個展覽每年舉辦一次。
2. 我們公司是有多年辦展經驗的展覽承辦企業。
3. 請問你們最近的展覽計畫是什麼？
4. 請問你們在展覽行銷方面的預算是多少？
5. 如果你願意的話，我可以為你介紹一下這個展覽。

E. Role-play

Practise the conversations according to the situations.

Situation 1

Mr. Smith is searching a place to hold an exhibition in Taiwan's home appliances company. He is talking with Mrs. Ding, a sales manager from a venue-searching agency, to get some information about o suitable place to stage the show.

Situation 2

Two persons are talking about planning an international exhibition(theme, guideline, time, location, expected participants, etc.). Please try the dialogue using your real names in pairs.

Situation 3

The Rainbow Exhibition Service is planning an air conditioner show which is expecting 500 exhibitors. Each exhibitor needs a standard booth(3m3m). Decide how much space you have to reserve from the exhibition center, and negotiate the price with the center. Please try the dialogue using your real names in pairs.

Situation 4

Rose Li is working for an exhibition organizing company. Now she is answering a phone call from Henry Smith who is from the organizing committee of a tradeshow.

Reference Answers

A. Specialized Terms

1.C   2.K   3.G   4.D   5.H   6.A   7.E   8.J
9.I   10.B

D. Speaking Up

1. The show is held annually.

2. Our company is an exhibition organizer with many years of experience in organizing exhibitions.

3. What are your plans for exhibitions recently?

4. What is your budget for exhibition marketing?

5. I can brief you on the exhibition if you like.

Chapter 4
Providing Exhibit Information 提供展覽資訊

Go over and expressions the following words.

1 tantamount		a.	等價
2 astounding		a.	令人驚駭的
3 meteoric		a.	流星的，輝煌而短暫的
4 proprietary		a.	所有的，私人擁有的
5 down payment			預付定金
6. megaevents			超大型會展、節慶、賽事活動

Section 1
Interpretation Activities

A. Sentence Interpretation

1. First, find out the equivalents of the following words.

virtually		導航路線	
target audience		電子文獻	
gauge		超媒體	
exhibitors manual		獲取	

2. Read the following to your partner for him or her to put them down in Chinese or English.

1. Information presented virtually could then also be used for educational purposes.

2. Obtain a list of exhibitors from the organizer, to determine

whether the show covers your particular industry.

3. Obtain a list of show visitors from the organizer, to see if the visitors are your target audience.

4. Speak to companies who exhibited at the last show, to gauge how successful it was.

5. Read your exhibitors manual carefully. You will find all the information you need to make ordering things easy.

6. 虛擬展覽由數條路線構成。

7. 真實展覽與虛擬展覽兩種展覽方式各有千秋。

8. 資源中心圖書館收集了會議與活動管理所需的資訊。

9. 資源圖書館裡的有些資訊必須得到 ACCA 辦公室同意方可進入，但我們也提供越來越多的電子文獻，您可以立刻獲取。

10. 超媒體的可能性允許我們以一種嶄新的方式展示展品的文化背景。

B. Passage Interpretation

1. First, find out the equivalents of the following words.

information technology.	
明確的優勢	
真實性	
虛擬展覽	
適合	

2. Read the following passages to yourself and render them

into Chinese or English.

Passage 1

Information has value and ought to be organized and managed like other organizational resources. Information management can be defined as: the effective management of the information resources (internal and external) of an organization through the proper application of information technology. Convention and exhibition industry is at a certain extent a kind of information industry in which the importance of information management appear clearer.

Your Answer

_____

_____

_____

_____

_____

_____

_____

_____

_____

_____

Passage 2

　　虛擬和現實兩種展覽方式夠各有其明確的優勢。兩種展覽中的展品是相同的，但適合它們的具體展示方法卻各不相同。現實展覽取決於展品的真實性，而虛擬展覽卻提供了一種把有關展品的不同資訊連結起來的可能。

Your Answer

_____

_____

_____

_____

_____

_____

_____

_____

_____

Reference Answers

A. Sentence Interpretation

1. words

virtually	以虛擬方式	導航路線	lines of navigation
target audience	目標觀眾	電子文獻	electronic document
gauge	評估	超媒體	hypermedia
exhibitors manual	參展商手冊	獲取	access

2. sentences

1. 以虛擬方式展示的資訊還具有教育的用途。

2. 從主辦方那裡獲取一張參展商名單，以便確定展覽是否涵蓋您的商業領域。

3. 從展覽主辦方那裡要一份展覽觀眾名錄，以便確定這些觀眾是否是您的目標觀眾。

4. 與上次參展的公司交流，評估展覽的成功程度。

5. 認真閱讀您的參展商手冊。您會發現裡面有方便您訂購東西所需的所有資訊。

6. The virtual exhibition comprises several lines of navigation.

7. Each of the two kinds of exhibitions, virtual and real, has its specific strengths.

8. The Resource Center Library is a collection of information pertaining to conference and event management.

9. Some of the information from the Resource Library must be requested from the ACCA office, but we have a growing number of electronic documents that you can access immediately.

10. The possibilities of hypermedia allow a new way of presenting an exhibit in its cultural context.

B. Passage Interpretation

1. words

information technology.	資訊技術
明確的優勢	specific strength
真實性	authenticity
虛擬展覽	virtual exhibition
適合	adopt to

2. paragraph

▌Passage 1

　　資訊是具有價值的資源，它應該和其他資源一樣得到統整和管理。資訊管理可以被定義為：透過正確應用資訊技術使一個團體的資訊資源（內部和外部資源）得以有效管理。會議和展覽業在某種程度上可以說是一種資訊產業。資訊資源管理因而更顯重要。

▌Passage 2

　　Each of the two kinds of exhibitions, virtual and real, has its specific strengths. Both exhibitions deal with the same objects, but present them in a way that is specifically adapted to the respective medium. While the real exhibition depends on the authenticity of the objects, the virtual one offers the possibility to interlink different pieces of information.

Section 2
Speaking Activities

A. Specialized Terms

Match the expressions on the left with the best Chinese equivalent on the right.

1. exhibition directory   A. 服務指南

2. exhibit prospectus   B. 半島形展位

3. gross square feet   C. 總面積

4. booth number   D. 攤位號碼

5. corner booth   E. 角落展位

6. island booth   F. 產品資訊表

7. peninsula booth   G. 護照申請表

8. service kit   H. 展位租金

9. space rate   I. 貴賓參觀卡

10. product and brand information   J. 參觀指南

11. passport request form   K. 參展資訊指南

12. VIP visitor invitation   L. 島形展位

B. Sample Conversation

Read aloud.

Situation: The Auto Expo project manager of the Galaxy Exhibition Company is discussing the project comparative word done by the planning staff, Peter, Tom, Sam and Cherry.

Manager: Is everybody here? Yes, now begins our meeting. Today we shall focus on the project comparative work you've done earlier. Let's begin with Peter.

Peter: OK. Comparing all previous Auto Expos with our present project, the biggest difference is size. They had more exhibitors than those to be expected of ours. Take for example the Auto Sourcing Expo 2001, it had about 800 exhibitors.

Tom: And we won't be competitive in terms of venue. As it was, most of the Auto Expos were held in world-renowned exhibition centers, like Hanover.

Manager: What do you think of it, Sam?

Sam: I quite agree with them. In fact, there is one more point we cannot neglect. At the last Expo, the suppliers were all world leading automotive parts manufacturers.

Manager: You mean there will be fewer exhibitors to ours just because of our infamous venue?

Sam: Perhaps. Our revenue depends largely upon the number of exhibitors.

Cherry: But on the other hand, we can offer larger exhibition area. There'll be 6,000 square meters.

Manager: True. As one big advantage, the area is divided into

3 sections. Besides the sourcing and supplier exhibitor sections, we can also offer meeting rooms for the sourcing exhibitors.

Cherry: And adding to the competitiveness, sourcing exhibitors can be prearranged for one-on-one meetings with suppliers.

Manager: Right you are. Moreover, the reversed on-site purchasing allows the buyers to set up their own pavilions, while the suppliers are free to choose on site.

Cherry: Really. I'm just coming to that. The buyers exhibit products, images and blueprints by the most effective means, and the local suppliers can also display export-level products to meet multinational prospects with the lowest cost.

Sam: What smart ideas! We call it 'double-win'.

Manager: Yes. You can never overstate it.

Peter: So in this way, we will gain a lion's share by offering Good services.

Manager: You bet. Comparatively speaking, I believe our project is to achieve greater success than we expected. Work hard, ladies and gentlemen, our efforts will not be unfruitful.

C. Functional Expressions

Read aloud and practice with your partner.
Talking about similarities and differences

They had more exhibitors than those to be expected of ours.

Comparing all the previous Auto Expos, the biggest difference is size.

The Supertechnology Show is more expensive than Power Coating Europe.

There are four times as many exhibitors at CES as at Coating Europe.

Another difference is that these shows represent two separate markets for us.

The main similarity is that many of the big name companies will be exhibiting at both Expos.

What the buyer will achieve will equal to that at 30 traditional exhibitions.

Talking about advantages and disadvantages

And adding to the competitiveness, sourcing exhibitors can be prearranged for one-on-one meetings with suppliers.

One big advantage of exhibiting at ADIPEC is that we can meet retailers from all over the country.

As one big advantage, the area is divided into 3 sections.

But on the other hand, we can offer larger exhibition area.

And adding to the competitiveness, sourcing exhibitors can be prearranged for one-on-one meetings with suppliers.

The only drawback of ADIPEC is the cost. It's going to be quite expensive.

D. Speaking Up

Render the following into english by using as many language skills learnt as possible

1. 展覽的主辦者會提供每位參展者參展資訊手冊。

2. 參展手冊包含申請表和合約、說明展位數量和位置的展區攤位圖，以及展覽公司可提供的所有服務。

3. 對於展廳的設計者來說，到會展中心繪製展廳的比例圖，其意義不僅僅是對展廳做一個測量。

4. 如果將展覽廳內那些大柱子或其他支撐結構的干擾作用考慮進來，實際展位數量就會減少。

5. 根據專業展覽公司設計的圖樣，會議籌畫者能確定可以出租多少展位和幾種類型的展位。

E. Role-play

Practice the conversation in English according to the situation.

Situation

A: You are applying for the position of engineer of a convention center in Taipei. The prospective boss is asking you some questions about building a convention and exhibition information system. Try to give appropriate answers.

B: You are the manager of information department of a convention center in Taipei. You are interviewing a recruit applying for the position of an engineer. Ask some questions about building a convention and exhibition information system.

Reference Answers

A. Specialized Terms

1.J   2.K   3.C   4.D.   5.E   6.L   7.B   8.A
9.H   10.F   11.G   10.I

D. Speaking Up

1. The expo organizer should provide exhibition manual for each exhibitor.

2. Exhibition Manual contains registration form and contract, specifies the number of booths and the booth layout in the exhibit area, and offer services available to exhibitors.

3. For exhibit hall designers, drawing a scaled layout of the exhibition hall is more than measuring the hall.

4. Based on the layout provided by professinoal exhibition companies, meeting planners can determine how many and what type of stands to let.

Chapter 5
Visiting Foreign Exhibitors
拜會贊助商

Go over and expressions the following words.

starter home	起步房
promotional literature	促銷宣傳資料
contributed papers	提交論文
green house effect	溫室效應
shuttle bus	接駁車
boom	繁榮
spotlight	聚光燈
exhilarating	令人興奮的
diversity	多樣化
COMDEX (Computer Dealer's Expo)	電腦經銷商博覽會
EXPO COMM (Exposition of Communications)	國際通信展

Section 1
Interpretation Activities

A. Sentence Interpretation

1. First, find out the equivalents of the following words.

1 direct marketing		6 資料庫	

2 special interest media		7 回饋率	
3 news release		8 印刷媒體	
4 layout		9 促銷	
5 mega event		10 受眾	

2. Read the following to your partner for him or her to put them down in Chinese or English.

1. Promoting through the media can reach the widest audience quickly, but it may not be focused on or targeted at a certain group of people.

2. Both approaches will take time and money, but it is possible to get support from media in the form of stories about your event for free or low cost if your event is a large or major or important gathering for some industry.

3. News media may carry a story about your event if the event is special in some way. Send a press release to the media telling them why your event is the first or biggest of its kind, or the most important in your industry.

4. You advertisement needs to be edited, the language checked and double-checked for errors, and the design checked for layout clarity and key information.

5. Response rates will depend on the interest level of the target, the beauty and suitability of the direct marketing piece, and the timing of the delivery to the target person or group.

6. 直接推廣方式則非常集中和具針對性，可以使目標人群看到你傳遞的資訊，但是這種方式成本較高，而且需要時間去處理。

7. 如果你已經有或能夠建立自己的聯絡資料資料庫，這可能
　　是推廣活動的最佳方式，而且得到的回應率也是最高的。

8. 如今的媒體包括印刷品、電臺、電視臺和網際網路。兩種
　　主要媒體分別是新聞和專業行業媒體。

9. 專業行業媒體有多種形式，例如行業雜誌，宣傳所屬行業
　　的電視或電臺節目，或專注於所屬行業或利益集團的網
　　站等。

10. 如今透過電子郵件形式直接推廣最為普遍，但必須確保目
　　標讀者同意接收經篩選的此類資訊。

B. Passage Interpretation

1. First, find out the equivalents of the following words.

potential revenue stream	
inventory	
統計特徵	
投資回報	

2. Read the following passages to yourself and render them into Chinese or English.

Passage 1

　　From an event's perspective, sponsorship often (but not always) represents a significant potential revenue stream. Yet, sponsorship are fast becoming business partnerships that offer resources beyond money. To succeed in the sponsorship stakes, event organizers must thoughtfully develop policies and strategies, providing a clear framework for both events and sponsors to decide on the value and suitability of potential partnerships. Having an inventory of the event assets available for sale is an important starting point for those seeking sponsorship.

Your Answer

_____

_____

_____

_____

_____

_____

_____

_____

Passage 2

在說服一家企業贊助活動時,了解其市場和目標是至關重要的。企業客戶的潛在客戶統計數據應該與活動參與者的統計特徵相一致。做好準備,向企業準確地說明其(贊助的)投資回報。如果你能表現出理解企業的需求,企業方面會更加願意傾聽活動是如何滿足這些需求的。

Your Answer

_____

_____

_____

_____

_____

_____

_____

_____

Reference Answers

A. Sentence Interpretation

1. words

1 direct marketing	直接行銷
2 special interest media	專業行業媒體
3 news release	新聞發布稿
4 layout	版面設計 / 布局圖
5 mega event	特大活動
6 資料庫	database
7 回饋率	response rate

8 印刷媒體	print media
9 促銷	promotion
10 受眾	audience

2. sentences

1. 透過媒體推廣可以迅速接觸到最廣泛的受眾，但是可能會不集中或沒有針對一個特定的人群。

2. 兩種方式都需要花費時間和金錢。但是，如果是規模龐大的活動或是某個行業的重要盛會，那麼你也許會得到媒體的支持，媒體會免費或低價為活動作宣傳。

3. 如果活動在某方面有特別之處，新聞媒體可能會對其進行報導。向媒體發布新聞稿，告訴他們本次活動在同類活動中堪稱首次或規模最大的理由。

4. 廣告需要編輯，語言需要校對、校對、再校對以避免錯誤，布局圖和重要資訊需要設計核對。

5. 回應率的高低取決於直接推廣文案的針對性、美觀性和適用性，以及向受眾發送時機的準確與否。應用這種動態發展的技術，以使你的活動在整個二十一世紀始終保持競爭力。

6. Direct marketing can be very focused on and targeted at the group you want to see your message, but it can be quite expensive and take time to set up well.

7. If you have or can build your own database of contacts interested in your event, this will probably be the best way to promote your event and will result in the highest response

rate.

8. Media Includes print, radio, television, and the Internet now. Two main kinds of media are news, and special interest media.

9. Special interest media come in all kinds. Magazines about your industry, TV or radio programs relating to your industry, or Web sites devoted to your industry or interest group are all examples.

10. Direct marketing by email is now the most popular, but make sure your target agrees to receive the messages through an opt-in list.

B. Passage Interpretation

1. words

potential revenue stream	潛在收入來源
inventory	詳細目錄
統計特徵	demographics
投資回報	return on investment

2. paragraph

█ Passage 1

　　從活動的角度來看，贊助往往（但不總是）代表著巨大的潛在收入來源。不過，贊助越來越成為一種商業合作行為，即贊助的是資源而不僅僅是錢。為成功地獲得贊助，活動主辦方必須制訂完善的方針和戰略，為活動和贊助商確立清晰的合作框架，以明確合作的價值和可行性。有成形的活動可供銷售，是尋求贊助的重要起點。

▌Passage 2

When convincing a company to sponsor your event, it's critical that you know their market and their goals. The demographics of their potential customers should match the demographics of your attendees. Be prepared to explain exactly what they can expect in return for their investment. If you can show them that you can understand their needs, they'll be more willing to listen to how your event support those needs.

Section 2
Speaking Activities

A. Specialized Terms

Match the expressions on the left with the best Chinese equivalent on the right.

1. open days(time, period)	A. 保全人員
2. rental charge	B. 標準裝配
3. subject	C. 地面負荷
4. hospitality	D. 獨立展覽

5. booth area	E. 公用設施服務
6. floor plan	F. 公展期
7. floor loading(covering)	G. 過道寬度
8. aisle width	H. 接待 / 招待
9. main dimension	I. 平面圖
10. standard fitting	J. 展位面積
11. security	K. 整體規格
12. free-standing exhibits	L. 主題 / 被調查者
13. access	M. 准入
14. utility service	N. 租金

B. Sample Conversation

Read aloud.

Situation: Mr. Li and Mrs. Ding are talking about the sponsorship package for the 2nd International Toy Exhibition.

Woman:　Good morning. What a pleasure to see you again, Mr. Li.

Man:　Good morning, Mrs. Ding. Nice to meet you too. It's said you are organizing the 2nd International Toy Exhibition .

Woman:　Yes, and that's why I come here. To be frank, we are seeking some sponsors now. Are you interested in it?

Man:　Well, we sponsored the 1st International Toy Exhibition last year, and really got a lot. Many consumers recognized our products and brand although we were a newly founded toy company at that time.

Woman: Yes, we cooperated with each other very well. So you are our fist choice for sponsors this time .

Man: Good. Would you please tell me some details about this year's exhibition? What are your objectives?

Woman: Here is the sponsorship package. In general, we hope to have 600 domestic and 400 international exhibitors this time, and attract about 10,000 visitors.

Man: Sounds wonderful. I will read this package in detail later. By the way, are there any other sponsors involved?

Woman: Actually, we try to cooperate with different kinds of sponsors according to their interest and levels of contribution.

Man: How much money is requested for title sponsor?

Woman: 500,000 NT dollars.

Man: That's really reasonable. Thank you very much for the information. I have to talk this with my teammates and let you know our decision in two weeks.

Woman: I really appreciate that. If you have any question, please do not hesitate to contact me.

Man: We will. Thanks again. Goodbye.

Woman: Goodbye. Thanks for your time.

C. Functional Expressions

Read aloud and practice with your partner.

How to elicit questions politely	Response
Can I help you?	Yes, I'd like to know some general information about your event
May I help you?	Yes, we'd like to know your sponsorship selection criteria.
Is there anything else I can do for you?	How to complete the sponsorship application form?

Frequently asked questions by potential sponsors

How much money is requested?

How will it be spent?

How many people will be present at the event?

What are the target audience for your event (for example, age, gender, employment statue, etc)?

How will the event be promoted?

Has the event been conducted in the past?

Do you intend repeating this event?

D. Speaking Up

Render the following into English by using as many language skills learnt as possible.

1. 贊助商冠名需多少錢？

2. 有多少人參加這次活動？

3. 請問還有什麼我可以幫忙的嗎？

4. 請問活動的目標。

5. 市場是怎樣的？

E. Role-play

Practice the conversations according to the situations.

Situation 1

Mr. Smith is from a company who would like to take part in the sponsorship of a show. Mrs. Li is the show manager. They are talking about what items the company chooses to sponsor and in return, what benefits the company is likely to obtain. Please try the dialogue with your partner.

Situation 2

Two companies sponsored a volunteer effort to clean up the city's park. Two persons from the companies are discussing this event.

Situation 3

Two employees from two companies who have sponsored a meeting on information technology, are discussing what their companies contributed to the meeting and how they feel about the decisions of their respective company. Please try the dialogue using your real names in pairs.

> **Situation 4**

Rose is working at the Sunshine Convention Service. Now she is answering a phone call from Henry Smith who wants to get some information about sponsoring a meeting.

Refenecne Answer

A. Specialized Terms

1.F   2.N   3.L   4.H   5.J   6.I   7.C   8.G
9.K   10.B.   11.A   12.D   13.M   14.E

D. Speaking Up

1. How much money is requested for title sponsors?

2. How many people will participating in this event?

3. Is there anything else I can do for you?

4. What are the goal of your event?

5. What are the target audience for your event?

Chapter 6

Negotiating on Exhibiting Space 展位談判

Go over and expressions the following words.

reliable	a.	可靠的
cater	v.	承辦（宴席）
skeptic	a.	懷疑的
constraint	n.	制約因素
liability	n.	責任
impose	v.	強加於
household utensil		家用器皿
forwarder	n.	運輸公司
warehouse	n.	倉庫
get acquainted with		熟悉
press conference		新聞發布會
Hannover		漢諾威（城市名）

Section 1
Interpretation Activities

A. Sentence Interpretation

1. First, find out the equivalents of the following words.

1 newsletter		6 高消費階層的	
2 target market		7 名人	
3 public relations		8 廣告宣傳品	
4 collateral material		9 新聞發布	

5 premium		10 戶外廣告	

2. Read the following to your partner for him or her to put them down in Chinese or English.

1. 才過一個月你的租場費就高出 25%。

2. 這並不意外。你也知道現在是展覽旺季。展覽公司都爭著租用我們的展覽館。

3. 但是你們的價格和我從其他地方得到的價格相比還是高出許多。

4. 可是我們場地交通便利，而且還有全市面積最大的底樓展廳。

5. 是的，這我承認。然而，我覺得很難在這麼高的價格上說服參展商購買攤位。

6. 那麼，你認為什麼樣的價格是可以接受的呢？

7. 我覺得應該再降價 15%。

8. 考慮到我們以往的良好合作，我們給你 10% 的優惠吧。

9. 好吧，我們就成交了。

B. Passage Interpretation

1. First, find out the equivalents of the following words.

fam. trip		指定服務商	
proceed		裝潢公司	
installation		招攬生意	
move-in		聊勝於無	

2. Read the following passages and translate them into Chinese or English.

Passage 1

L: Good morning, Mr. Smith. I hope you enjoyed your fam. trip yesterday.

S: Good morning, Mr. Li. I did enjoy it. It was a wonderful trip.

L: I'm very glad to hear that. I suspect, however, we'd like to get down to business. How would you like to proceed with the negotiations?

S: Today, I would like to talk about the move-in with you. We have a plan to attend this exhibition organized by your company, but we still want to confirm some terms about move-in.

L: What terms do you want to confirm?

S: When are we supposed to finish the installation?

L: All exhibits must be constructed and decorated by 5 p.m. on the day before exhibit opening.

S: That's what we worry about. Because we might need to spend some time decorating the stand. The time limit is tense. Shall we move in earlier or finish it later?

L: That doesn't conform to our usual practice. Anyway, could you tell me how much earlier you want to move in?

S: 2 hours.

Passage 2

L: 兩個小時太多了。 我們無法接受。

S: 那多長時間是可以的呢？

L: 我們只能給半個小時。

S: 半個小時？太少了。

L: 我知道，可是這已經是我們公司規定內的可以做出最大讓步了。

S: 好吧！總比沒有好。我們會儘量在規定的時間內完成的。 第二個我們想確定的是關於裝潢公司的事情。根據展覽會的相關條款，你們公司指定了 FREEMAN 裝潢公司，那麼我們可以帶我們自己的裝潢工人入場嗎？

L: 可以。但是你們的工人任何時間都不能在場館內招攬生意。你們要對他們的行為負責。

S: 我明白你們的意思。

Reference Answers

A. Sentence Interpretation

1. words

1 newsletter	時事通訊
2 target market	目標市場
3 public relations	公共關係
4 collateral material	輔助宣傳材料
5 premium	贈品
6 高消費階層的	upscale

7 名人	celebrity
8 廣告宣傳品	advertising specialty
9 新聞發布	news release
10 戶外廣告	outdoor advertising

2. sentences

1. Your venue rental rate is 25% higher than that one month ago.

2. There is no surprise. You know, it is the peak season of exhibitions. Exhibition companies are now all applying for spaces in our venue.

3. But your prices are still much higher than what we are offered by other venues.

4. As you can see, we are easily accessible and have this city's largest display area on the ground floor.

5. I know that's true. However, it will be hard for us to talk exhibitors into renting spaces of such a high price.

6. Could you tell me your idea of a reasonable price?

7. I think there should be another 15% discount.

8. For a good start of our potential cooperation in the future, we can give you another 10% discount.

9. OK. That's the deal.

B. Passage Interpretation

1. words

fam. trip	現場考察	指定服務商	official service contractor
proceed	繼續	裝潢公司	Decorating company
installation	搭建	招攬生意	solicit business
move-in	進展	總比沒有好	Better than nothing

2. paragraph

▌Passage 1

L: 史密斯先生，早安。希望您喜歡昨天的實地考察旅行。

S: 李先生，早安。我非常喜歡。這是一次很美好的旅行。

L: 我很高興你能喜歡。我想我們應該坐下來談生意了。你認為我們今天談什麼呢？

S: 今天我想跟你們談談關於布展的事情。我們計劃參加此次你們公司主辦的展覽，可是我們還要確認一些關於布展的條款。

L: 你們想確認的是什麼條款？

S: 我們什麼時候就要完成布展？

L: 所有的展臺必須在展覽正式開始的前一天下午五點之前布置完畢。

S: 這正是我們擔心的。因為我們可能需要點時間來裝飾我們的展臺。你們的時間限制太緊張了。我們是否可以提前進場或者延遲退場的時間呢？

L: 這不符合我們慣有的做法。不過，你們可以先告訴我你們想提前多長時間入場？

S: 兩個小時。

Passage 2

L: Two hours is too much! I don't think it is acceptable.

S: How much is possible?

L: What we can do is to offer half an hour.

S: Half an hour? That's little.

L: I know, but that is what we can do according to this exhibition rules.

S: Ok. Better than nothing. The second term we want to confirm is about the decorating company. According to the rules, your company has selected Freeman Decorating Company as the official service contractor. Can we take our decorating workers in?

L: Yes, you can. But your workers may not solicit business in the exhibit hall at any time. You must be responsible for the actions of them.

S: I see what you mean.

Section 2
Speaking Activities

A. Specialized Terms

Match the expressions on the left with the best Chinese equivalent on the right.

1. offer	A. 還價
2. counter offer	B. 實盤
3. rock-bottom/floor price	C. 報價

4. firm offer	D. 底價
5. transaction	E. 展出淨面積
6. call off (the deal)	F. 優惠條件
7. inquiry	G. 詢價
8. best terms	H. 特殊裝修地展位
9. quotations	I. 做出讓步
10. make concessions	J. 不做（這筆）生意
11. exhibition net area	K. 生意
12.raw space with special decoration	L. 報盤

B. Sample Conversation

Read aloud.

Situation: Li-Ming of the local exhibition center receives the Auto Expo project manager of the Galaxy Exhibition Company. The manager intends to discuss the price terms for reserving exhibition area with Mr. Li-Ming.

Li-Ming: Hello, Mr. Thompson. It's a pleasure to see you again so soon.

Manager: It's my pleasure to see you again, too. Mr. Li.

Li-Ming: Take a seat, please.

Manager: Thank you.

Li-Ming: Do you care for tea or coffee?

Manager: Tea, please. Thanks. Shall we get down to business right now?

Li-Ming: OK. I believe you have received our center's size catalogue and price list.

Manager: Yes, we have given it serious considerations and today I've come for the details about price terms. We found your price on the high side.

Li-Ming: I'm surprised to hear that. I think our prices are competitive. Hardly can you get such favorable prices from other exhibition centers.

Manager: Perhaps you are right. But it's really hard for us to rent it to our exhibitors at such a high price.

Li-Ming: What's your proposal then?

Manager: I suggest that there be 15% discount.

Li-Ming: What's the total area you have in your mind?

Manager: About 5,500 square meters.

Li-Ming: Which halls are you interested in?

Manager: They must be the Center Hall and its side rooms on the 1st floor, the entire second floor of No.1 Eastern Hall.

Li-Ming: 5,500 square meters is certainly not a large area. But since it is the first business between you and us, you may have our 5% reduction.

Manager: It's impossible for me to accept that. Can we meet it halfway: a reduction of 10%?

Li-Ming: Your counter offer is not acceptable. We have never offered that before.

Manager: Well, if you insist, can you prolong the hall closing hours from 6:00p.m. to 7:30p.m.during the event free of charge?

Li-Ming: Yes, we can keep the hall open half an hour longer. For a good start to our business relationship, we'll give you 5% discount and the free use of the halls from 6:00p.m. to 7:30p.m. during the event.

Manager: OK. Let's call it a deal.

C. Functional Expressions

Read aloud and practice with your partner.

Saying the prices offered are too high

We find your prices are on the high side.

Your price is much higher than we were expecting to pay.

Your price is not so attractive as that offered by other suppliers.

Your price is out of line with the current market price.

I'm so surprised to see that your price is almost 20% higher than last year's.

Asking for a counter offer

Would you let us know your counter offer?

What reasonable price do you have in your mind?

What is your proposal?

What do you think is a completive price?

Could you tell me your idea of a reasonable price?

Bargaining for a lower price

Can we meet it halfway: a reduction of 10%?

If you consider reducing the rental rates, I'll reserve a greater amount of exhibition space.

If you insist on not making a discount, I can find lower prices elsewhere.

Agreeing to reduce the price

Since it is the first business between you and us, you may have our 5% reduction.

For a good start to our business relationship, we'll give you 5% discount and the free use of the halls from 6:00 p.m. to 7:30 p.m. during the event.

In view of our cooperation in the past, we accept your counter-offer.

To encourage future business, we'll make an exception and give you a 8% discount.

If you reserve enough large exhibition space, we're preparing to reduce the price by 8%.

Refusing to reduce the price

Your counter offer is not acceptable. We have never offered that before.

We have offered you our rock-bottom price. We can't make any further concessions.

I'm afraid there is no room to negotiate the price.

This is really our floor price. If you can't accept it, I'm afraid we have to call the deal off.

D. Speaking Up

Understand the speaker's intention, and then fill in the blanks.

1. ——I believe you've studied out catalogue and price. Are you interested in some of our exhibition halls?

   —— _____.

   （用意：表示對方價格太高）

2. —— _____?

   （用意：請對方還價）

   ——I think you should at least reduce the rental by 15%

3. ——The best I can do is to give you a 10% discount.

   —— _____.

   （用意：表示難以接受對方條款）

4. ——18% is impossible for me to accept. That will leave no margin for profit.

   —— _____.

   （用意：說服對方降價）

5. ——To conclude the deal, I'd say a reduction of at least 25% would help.

   —— _____.

   （用意：拒絕成交）

E. Role-play

Practise the conversations acoording to the situations.

Situation 1

The Galaxy Exhibition Company is planning an AgroExpo that is expecting 600 exhibitors. Each need a standard pavilion(10m*10m). Decide how much space you have to reserve from the exhibition center, and negotiate the price terms with the exhibition center. With your partner, act out the Dialogue using the skills you have just learnt in this unit.

Situation 2

You are an exhibitor from Australia. You are calling to hire a stand. You want to know whether you still stand a chance to have a stand near the main entrance.

You are working as a receptionist in Taipei World Trade Center. Tell the exhibitor that there are some stands of his kind left.

Situation 3

You are an exhibitor from Great Britain. You are calling to hire a stand. You want to the size of stand areas and the possibility of designing you own stands.

You are working as a receptionist in Taipei World Trade Center. Tell the exhibitor that the size of stand areas is of average standard.

Refenence Answer

A. Specialized Terms

1.C   2.A   3.D   4.B   5.K   6.J   7.G   8.F
9.L   10 I   11.E   12.H

D. Speaking Up

1. If you consider reducing the rental rates, I'll reserve a greater amount of exhibition space.

2. Would you let us know your counter offer?

3. Your price is still out of line with the current market price.

4. If you insist on not making a discount, I can find lower prices elsewhere.

5. I'm afraid there is no room to negotiate the price.

Chapter 7
Hiring A Stand 申請展位

Go over and expressions the following words.

summit		n.	峰會
commemorate		v.	紀念
peak period			旺季
mammoth-sized		a.	大型的
brochure		n.	小冊子
supervisor		n.	主管
scheme		n.	方案，計畫

Section 1
Interpretation Activities

A. Sentecce Interpretation

1. First, find out the equivalents of the following words.

licensed	有資質的
presentation aid	演示輔助工具
distraction	干擾物
煙火展示	Firework display
易燃物品	flammable substance
加強管理	control carefully

2. Read the following to your partner for him or her to put them down in Chinese or English.

1. Location preparation is made up of many points related to the specific conditions of the venue: when you get it, and what you will need it for.

2. Venue management companies should insist that their customers use licensed, insured, and reputable engineering companies to install their decorations if they are out of the ordinary.

3. If the decoration will use a large amount of electricity for huge light displays, there should be an extra electricity charge included in the contract.

4. Most formal meetings have groups on both sides of a table, sitting in chairs and probably using presentation aids of some kind.

5. The table should be a standard height, with no distractions in the middle like plants that will stop one side seeing the other.

6. 根據安排的活動種類的不同，場館準備也將有所不同。

7. 裝飾工作大部分取決於會展管理公司，但是還有許多關鍵要點也需要有場館管理公司參與。

8. 因此，對於這些煙火裝置以及其他易燃物品應加強管理。

9. 只要服務良好，他們通常會再度光臨。

10. 在會議過程中為商務人士提供所需的服務非常重要。

B. Passage Interpretation

1. First, find out the equivalents of the following words.

accessibility	容易得到
amenities	娛樂設施
revitalization	恢復元氣
Messe	德國展覽中心
periphery	周邊地區
Frankfurt	法蘭克福
Glasgow	格拉斯哥
insufficient car parking	停車場不足
congested road access	道路擁擠
Cologne	科隆
單獨使用	used independently
按專業目標建造的	purpose-built

2. Read the following passages to yourself and render them into Chinese or English.

Passage 1

At the level of the urban region there is often a debate to best location for an exhibition centre. A central site near the city centre provides the facility with good accessibility by public transport, and access to the varied amenities of the downtown zone, including hotels and night life, and assists with the revitalization of the inner city. Early twentieth-century Messe, such as those of Cologne and Frankfurt are in fact centrally located, but later centres are likely to have found inner city is in decay, such as in Glasgow, has it been possible to build an exhibition centre in the central area. Inner city sites may have problems with insufficient car parking and congested road access. Frequently it has been necessary to choose a site on the periphery where undeveloped land was available with good communications and at low cost.

Your Answer

_____
_____
_____
_____
_____
_____
_____
_____

Passage 2

　　展覽在寬敞的大廳裡舉行，一個展覽中心通常由一系列相連接的大廳組成，它們既能單獨使用，又能合併後一起使用。盛大的展覽中心可同時進行多項展覽活動。現在，大多數展覽中心是按專業目標建造的。它們也有室外場地。有一種專業的展覽場地是農業交易會，他們主要是在室外展出。展覽中心也需有提供餐飲的設施或辦公室。近年來，展覽中心已經開始提供會議室，因為會議常常與展覽連繫在一起的。有時，這些會議在展覽中心附近的飯店裡召開。

Your Answer

_____

_____

_____

_____

_____

_____

_____

_____

_____

Reference Answers

A. Sentecce Interpretation

1. 場地準備由很多點組成，與場地的具體情況有關：什麼時候拿到的，需要做什麼。

2. 場地管理公司應堅持要求客戶：如果他們是與眾不同的，那麼他們應聘用有執照、有保險、有信譽的工程公司進行裝修。

3. 如果裝飾需要大量用電做大型的燈光展示，在合約中就會包括需要額外支付的電費。

4. 在大多數的正式會議中，人們坐在會議桌兩邊就座，可能還會使用某種演示輔助工具。

5. 桌子的高度應為標準高度，中間不能擺放諸如盆景那樣的東西，因為這些東西容易分散人們的注意力，還會擋住與會者的視線，使得彼此看不清對方。

6. Location preparation will be different depending on the kind of event you are managing.

7. Decoration is largely up to the event management company, but there are many points the venue management company will also be involved in.

8. The Use of these firework displays and other flammable substances should be controlled carefully.

9. They usually will go back again and again as long as the service is good.

10. It is important to serve the needs of business people while they are holding their meetings.

B. Passage Interpretation

Passage 1

　　在市區，為展覽中心選一個最佳會址常會引起爭論。靠近市中心的地方，乘公車容易到達，接近繁華商業區的各種令人愉快的環境，如飯店和夜生活，有助於恢復城市的活力。20 世紀初期的德國展覽中心，如科隆和法蘭克福的展覽中心，實際定位於市中心。但是，後來發現展覽中心定在發達的市內，費用太貴。只有在城內，如格拉斯哥尚有餘輝的地區，建一個展覽中心才可能。但城內可能有停車場不足和道路擁擠的問題，有必要將展覽中心選在不太發達的周邊地區。那裡交通好，費用低。

Passage 2

Exhibitions are held in large halls, and an exhibition centre usually consists of a series of linked halls which can be used either independently or in combination. Very largely exhibiton centres may host more than one event at the same time. Today most exhibition centres are purpose-built. They also have space outside. A specialist type of showground is the agricultural fair ground, which is mainly outdoor display space. Exhibition centres also require catering facilities and perhaps office space. In recent years exhibition centres have begun to provide rooms for meetings, sInce conferences often take place in association with shows. Sometimes these conferences take place in hotels which have been built nearby.

Section 2
Speaking Activities

A. Specialized Terms

Match the expressions on the left with the best Chinese equivalent on the right.

1. stand   A. 單獨設計的展臺

2. booth   B. 歐式展棚

3. hire   C. 北美式展棚

4. book   D. 側廊

5. modular   E. 通道

6. shell stand   F. 框架 / 骨架組合單元

7. shell module keynotcr   G. 框架 / 骨架展臺 (只完成框架，內部由購買者自己裝修的展臺)

8. gangway   H. 有標準元件的

9. aisle   I. 預訂

10. north american booth   J. 租用

11. european shell scheme   K. 展棚

12. individual designed stand   L. 展臺

B. Sample Conversation

Read aloud.

Situation: Shirley White is calling to enquire about reserving a exhibit stand at the 22nd World Nursing Congress.

A: Hello, Information Department of International Exhibition & Convention Center. This is Hazel Brown speaking. Can I help you?

B: This is Shirley White speaking. I'm calling to make sure the arrangement when I am attending the 22nd World Nursing Congress.

A: Okay, Ms. White. We are ready to provide any convenience.

B: Thanks. I'm wondering if you can help me reserve a room from 23rd, the day before the congress until 28th, the last day of the congress.

A: Yes. You could have two choices: Hotel Marriott with a room rate of $100 and Radisson SAS Royal hotel of $120 per day.

B: Which one is nearer to the Congress Center?

A: I am afraid Radisson is nearer.

B: Then I'd like to take it. Besides, is there still any stand available for the exhibition during the Congress?

A: Let me check. Yes. We do have several stands left but quite far away from the entrance.

B: That is not important. How much is it if I hire a stand for one day to do some consulting and advertising for my nursing agency?

A: We give a 10% discount for the inner stands, that is $120 dollars per day.

B: Done. By the way, what's the weather like in Copenhagen?

A: It is the best season now in Copenhagen, neither too hot nor too cold. You should spare some time to do sightseeing when you're here.

B: Sure. Thank you for you help.

C. Functional Expressions

Read aloud and practice with your partner.

Talking about the booth size	Response
Can you explain to me the options of stands first?	We offer package stand and raw space.
What is the area for raw space?	The minimum area for one raw space indoor is twenty-seven square meters.
Are there any different sizes of booths?	Yes, there are two different sizes.
How large is the standard booth?	It's nine feet by ten feet.

Enquiring about booth price	Response
How much do you charge for the stands and raw space respectively?	The package stands cost at least 982,000 NT dollars per unit, equivalent to about 3,000 US dollars.
Does the price of the show included meals?	Yes, the cost of meals is included.

What is included in the price?	It covers the food and accommodations and the cost of a booth in the corner.
Are there any different costs for the package stands?	Yes. Costs vary with the different locations of the stand.
Do you cheaper ones?	Then you may choose corner stands.
What is least expensive booth you have?	We have a few spaces left in the back for 60,000 NT dollars.

Choosing booths locations

If the price is right, I'll take the booth in the center.

I will set up in the center if the price is reasonable.

If it doesn't cost too much I will choose the center location.

Bargaining for booth rentals	**Response**
Can you make a cut rate for me?	Sorry to say that we can't, but we can Increase the dimension of your space a little without Incurring extra fee.
Can you lower the price for the center booth?	I cannot lower the price for you, but I can make your space a little bit bigger.
Is it possible to reduce the price?	I can Increase the size of the spot, but I can't decrease the price.

What are the best terms of booth price?

I will enlarge your spot a little, but I will not drop the price.

D. Speaking Up

Render the following into English by using as many language skills learnt as possible.

1. 請問我的展位在哪裡？
2. 這是會場布置圖。我們現在的位置是服務臺，您的展位在這。
3. 我只想確定一下所有東西都已到位，並且沒有問題。
4. 我們一定要在下午一點之前布置好。
5. 我現在可以去看一看月臺和貨物嗎？

E. Role-play

Practise the conversation in English.

Part 1

A: 請問一個標準攤位的費用是多少？
B: 每個標準攤位是 1,800 美元。
A: 我並不需要整個攤位，只要一半就夠了。
B: 我剛好知道有另一家公司想要合用攤位。
A: 太好了。如果合用一個攤位的話，該付多少錢？
B: 你預付一半的費用。
A: 你能給我一些這個公司的資料嗎？

B: 我查到後再打電話給你，可以嗎？

A: 請儘快告訴我。

Part 2

● **Situation 1**

C. You are an exhibitor from Australia. You are calling to hire a stand. You want to know whether you still stand a chance to have a stand near the main entrance.

D. You are working as a receptionist in Taipei World Trade Center. Tell the exhibitor that there are some stands of his kind left.

● **Situation 2**

C. You are an exhibitor from Great Britain. You are calling to hire a stand. You want to the size of stand areas and the possibility of designing you own stands.

D. You are working as a receptionist in Taipei World Trade Center. Tell the exhibitor that the size of stand areas is of average standard.

Reference Answers

A. Specialized Terms

1.l   2.k   3.j   4.i   5.h   6.g   7.f   8.e
9.d   10.c   11.b   12.a

D. Speaking Up

1. Could you tell me where I can find my booth?

2. Here's a map of the exhibition hall, and here we are at the service desk. It is your booth.

3. I just want to be sure that everything is here and in working condition.

4. We really need to set up before 1:00 in the afternoon.

5. Do you think I could check on my booth and my goods now?

Chapter 8
Personal Sales Calls 銷售拜訪（電話）

Go over and expressions the following words.

1 deferment		n.	遷延，延期，暫緩
2. IC chips			智慧晶片
3. incorporate		v.	促進
4. mascot		n.	吉祥物
5.spec		n.	規格
6 counterfeit		v.	偽造，假冒
7 miniature		adj.	微型的
8 authenticate		v.	鑑別

Section 1
Interpretation Activities

A. Sentence Interpretation

1. First, find out the equivalents of the following words.

public relation breakthrough competitive marketing force 潛在群體 行銷策略	

2. Read the following to your partner for him or her to put them down in Chinese or English.

1. There is no question that the development of the Internet has become the most important communication and marketing media breakthrough since the printing press in the mid-fifteenth century.

2. It has been shown that those events that are close to inexpensive, safe public transportation or those events that feature closed-in reasonably priced parking will attract more guests than those that do not offer these amenities.

3. Advertising is what you say about your event, whereas public relation is what others are saying about your event.

4. In most cases, event managers use marketing forces such as advertising, public relations, promotion, advertising specialties, stunts, and other techniques to promote individual events.

5. The Internet will continue to drive the development of the global event management industry. You must use this dynamic technology quickly and accurately to ensure that your event remains competitive throughout the twenty-first century.

6. 在會展活動業中，目標市場這個術語的含義主要是指參加某一特定活動的潛在客群。

7. 選擇機場旅館，是因為這一場所飛進飛出的航班使與會者能夠花費最少的旅行時間，高效地完成工作。

8. 每一個會展活動都有其獨特性，即使並非如此，行銷人員也要努力把它表現成這樣。

9. 無論一項會展活動的性質如何，其成功與否都取決於採用何種行銷策略來吸引消費者。

10. 作為會展活動行銷的一個重要組成部分，市場調研和分析有助於行銷人士確定其目標市場的態度、期望及需求。

B. Passage Interpretation

1. First, find out the equivalents of the following words.

cyber brochureware static show-biz utilitarian brand recognition 營運成本 合理的活動價位 市場競爭分析	

2. Read the following passages to yourself and render them into Chinese or English.

Passage 1

Today, after experiencing five consistent years of cyber growth, event marketing specialists are speaking about second and third generations of Web sites. The first and least developed type of Web site is brochureware. Web sites of this type are static and contain basic information about an organization, including its address and services. The site reflects a paper brochure placed on the Web. The second group of Web sites is known as showbiz. These sites try to amuse visitors through interactive features, flashing pictures, news reports, or press reviews. The last and most developed type of Web sites are called utilitarian. These sites offer viewers a unique and balanced interactive service that is both highly informative and helpful in building brand recognition and loyalty.

Your Answer

_____

_____

_____

_____

_____

_____

_____

_____

Passage 2

　　市場調查能幫你確定價格。市場調研的部分內容是進行市場競爭分析，分析其他提供相似活動的團體。您最初可能認為您的產品與其他所有活動都截然不同。然而，在採訪潛在的購票者或客人時，您可能會驚訝地發現他們認為您的活動與許多其他活動相似。因此，你必須仔細一地列出所有競爭者的活動以及它們的價格，以幫助你確定一個合理的活動價位。一般來說，有兩個因素決定價格：營運成本和市場競爭。

Your Answer

_____

_____

_____

_____

_____

_____

_____

_____

_____

Reference Answer

A. Sentence Interpretation

1. words

public relation	公共關係
breakthrough	突破
competitive	有競爭力的
marketing force	行銷方式
潛在群體	potential group
行銷策略	marketing strategy

2. sentences

1. 毫無疑問，自十五世紀中葉印刷媒體發展以來，網際網路的發展已經成為在溝通和行銷媒介方面最重要的突破。

2. 據認為，那些毗鄰價廉且安全的公共交通工具的會展活動，以及那些擁有封閉和價格合理的停車場所的活動，比那些無法提供以上便利措施的活動，更加吸引消費者。

3. 廣告是你自己對於會展活動的宣傳，而公共關係是他人對於活動的看法。

4. 在大多數情況下，會展活動經理人採用廣告、公關、促銷、廣告宣傳品、驚險表演等行銷方式來推廣活動。

5. 網際網路將繼續推動全球活動管理業的發展。你必須迅速準確地應用這種動態發展的技術，以使你的活動在整個二十一世紀始終保持競爭力。

6. The term "target market" refers, in the main, to the people who would be coming to a particular event in the event industry.

7. Airport hotels are chosen because the fly-in fly-out design of the location enables the attendees to get the work done with the minimum travel time.

8. Every event is unique. Even if this may not be the case, at

least event marketers need to endeavor to present it as such.

9. Regardless of the nature of the event, its success largely depends on what marketing strategies are adopted to attract consumers.

10. As a key component of event marketing, market research and analysis helps the marketer to determine the attitudes, expectations and needs of the target market.

B. Passage Interpretation

1. words

cyber	電腦
brochureware	宣傳冊式網頁
static	靜態的
show-biz	娛樂新聞式網頁
utilitarian	專用型網頁
brand recognition	創造品牌認知度
營運成本	the cost of doing business
合理的活動價位	the appropriate price for your event.
市場競爭分析	competitive analysis study

2. paragraph

▌Passage 1

　　如今，在經歷了連續五年的電腦應用成長之後，會展活動行銷專家們正在探討第二代和第三代網頁。最早的也是最原始的網頁是宣傳冊式網頁。這種類型的網頁是靜態的，只包含一個團隊的基本資訊，如地址和服務專案。它就像把一個紙本的宣傳冊放在網頁上。第二種網頁是娛樂新聞式網頁，它採用互動、動畫、新聞報導、媒體評論的方式來愉悅訪問者。最新也是最發達的網頁類型是專用型網頁。它為訪問者提供一種獨特而穩定的互動式服務，其中既包含大量資訊，又有利於創造品牌認知度和忠誠度。

Passage 2

Market research will help you determine price. Part of this market research will include conducting a competitive analysis study of other organizations offering similar event products. You may initially believe that your product is uniquely different from every other event. However, when interview potential ticket buyers or guests you may be surprised to learn that they consider your event similar to many others. Therefore, you must carefully list all competing events and the prices being charged to help you determine the appropriate price for your event. Typically, two factors determine price, i.e., the cost of doing business and the marketplace competition.

Section 2
Speaking Activities

A. Specialized Terms

Match the expressions on the left with the best Chinese equivalent on the right.

1. personal sales call　　　　　　A. 集中銷售

2. trade show selling　　　　　　B. 未經預約的拜訪（或電話）

3. familiarization tour　　　　　　C. 現場視察

4. telephone sales call follow-up　　D. 展會銷售

5. cold call　　　　　　　　　　E. 開放性問題

6. sales blitzes　　　　　　　　　F. 電話銷售後續聯繫

7. screening prospects　　　　　　G. 篩選潛在客戶

8. telemarketing　　　　　　　　H. 個別拜訪（電話）銷售

9. open-ended question　　　　　　I. 電話推銷

10. destination marketing　　　　　J. 目的地銷售

B. Sample Conversation

Read aloud.

Situation: Su-Hui, sales clerk of the Claude Convention Center, is paying a personal sales call to a foreign-funded electronic enterprise. She is talking face to face with a prospect about convention sales.

Su-Hui: Good morning, Mr. Hilton. How is everything?

Hilton: Couldn't be better. Thanks. And you?

Su-Hui: Me too. Is any event you are planning for next year?

Hilton: Yes, we'll be having a new series of training sessions next year. Are you able to serve this event in your center?

Su-Hui: I'm delighted if our convention center can be of service to you. Now let me show you the floor plans and the map of the facilities. You can see how it can serve your future needs. I believe you would be very interested.

Hilton: I remember you have had new meeting facilities, right?

Su-Hui: Yes, you're right, Mr. Hilton. We are now building a specially-designed conference hall. It will open in 3 months' time. We'll be honored if we could come as our distinguished guest to a special opening reception and tour the weekend of October 21 to October 22.

Hilton: Thank you. I'd love to.

Su-Hui: Is it that each department in your company is to conduct its own training meetings? Could you tell me the size of the training party?

Hilton: We have 30 trainees.

Su-Hui: I'm sure I'll find our smaller multimedia rooms ideally

	meeting your needs.
Hilton:	You will not charge us for audio-visual equipment, will you?
Su-Hui:	If you are sure you could book 400 room nights, we can also let you have your opening reception free of charge.
Hilton:	My last meeting was totally spoiled (毀 壞 了) by those two incompetents on my staff who are supposed to handle all details and they made sure that all points were covered.
Su-Hui:	No worry, sir. We can solve your problem. We have just hired three experienced assistant convention managers. They would be happy to take up these service details for you.
Hilton:	That would be Good. I shall consult with the general manager about this. I'll see you to touch the details once we've decided.
Su-Hui:	Thank you, Mr. Hilton. We look forward to seeing you soon again.

C. Functional Expressions

Read aloud and practice with your partner.
Opening the sales call

Good afternoon, Mr. Hilton. I'm Su-Hui from the Claude International Convention Center, Taipei.

I've heard so much about what your firm has been doing in the area of printer technology and application. And I'm eager to hearing more about your innovation.

Would you be interested in learning how other associations used one of our theme parties to Increase attendance?

May I show you a few examples of our state-of-the –art audio-visual system?

Getting prospect involvement

Where did you have your incentive meeting?

How many training meetings do you stage each month?

What is your average attendance at your annual convention?

Why do you think last year's meeting was so successful?

What are the essential elements to you in selecting a meeting site?

Closing the sales call

Don't you think our audiovisual equipment will greatly en-hance your training sessions?

Don't you think our ballroom would make an elegant setting for your awards banquet?

Don't you find our golf course to be one of the finest in the state?

May I reserve space on a definite basis?

D. Role-play

Practise the conversations acoording to the situations.

Situation 1

A major U.S. ABC Computer Corporation is calling the Mandarin Oriental Hotel to get some information about the group prices of rooms and seasonal prices of rooms. In pairs, try the Dialogue using your real names. One person will be the assistant manager for ABC Computer Corporation. The other person will be the sales manager for the Mandarin Oriental Hotel.

Situation 2

Su-Hui was hired as a sales trainee a year ago, and was promoted to salesman after only six months. She has made good, but not outstanding, progress, meeting her sales quota by only slim margins. She is now beginning her second year of personal selling and wants to expand her current prospect list by making cold calls. Try to give Su-Hui some suggestions about the skills of making cold calls. One person plays the role of Su-Hui. The other is you.

Reference Answer

A. Specialized Terms

1.H   2.D   3.C   4.F   5.B   6.A   7.G   .8I

9.E   10.J

Chapter 9

Hiring People and Loaning Properties 租借物品 / 租用人員

Go over and expressions the following words.

1 billboard		n.	布告板，看板
2 fragile		adj.	易碎的，脆的
3 horologe		n.	鐘錶
4 foster		V.	撫育，培養，鼓勵
5 FPA	平安險		
6.WPA	Wi-Fi 存取保護		
7.breakage risk	破碎險		
8.all risk	一切險		

Section 1
Interpretation Activities

A. Sentence Interpretation

1. First, find out the equivalents of the following words.

prioritize	分出輕重緩急
coordinator	管理協調人員
uniform colors	有特定顏色的制服
theming some meal	主題化餐飲
常常談論的一個問題	frequently discussed issues
非常重要	count
想客人之所想	guest obsesse

2. Read the following to your partner for him or her to put

them down in Chinese or English.

1. There are so many things you should bear in mind, so to prioritize your activities, check for any last minute changes, notes left for you, correspondence, phone messages or e-mails.

2. A check can be made of arrangements between coordinator and staff to deal with any final requests or changes to the booked details.

3. Staff is easy to identify by uniform colors or with visible ID that can be worn around the neck.

4. One thing that can't follow you around is the deliveries of supplies.

5. There is a trend towards theming some meals during events, which combines entertainment with good food and drink.

6. 關於會議管理常常談論的一個問題是，銷售人員在服務過程中到底應該做些什麼。

7. 展會的工作人員提供服務，參展商或與會者享受服務。兩者之間，後者對展會的期望如何是非常重要的。

8. 我們要使我們的員工的服務比客人期望的要好，讓員工想客人之所想。

9. 隨著準備工作的進一步就緒，各式各樣的物品將被運送到位。

10. 展覽會和展銷會成功的一點是它能吸引足夠多的參展商來滿足參觀者的需要，同時能夠吸引足夠多的參觀者來滿足參展商的目的。

B. Passage Interpretation

1. First, find out the equivalents of the following words.

logistics	物流業務
distributed	分送
deadlines	最後日期
central arrival point	集中收貨區
flow of crew around the venue	工作人員在展館的流動
投影設備	video projection
調試設備	test their material
音箱效果	sound reinforcement
電腦文本	computer-generated text
構圖	graphics
圖像轉換	transfer of pictures

2. Read the following passages to yourself and render them into Chinese or English.

Passage 1

Logistics is the discipline of planning and organizing the flow of goods, equipment and people. Logistics includes ticketing and enquiries, arrival and departure of visitors as well as the flow of crew around the venue. Within logistics, the preparation, opening and running of an event depends on getting all the elements to the right place in time for a range of deadlines. This can be a complicated process and individual staff and departments will be expected to work with each other to get their own list of requirements prepared. And when events are being run, the convention and exhibition organizer should make sure that everything goes smoothly. Supplies can be ordered and delivery checked, usually at the central arrival point, and the supplies distributed as required to the places where they are needed.

Your Answer

_____

_____

_____

_____

_____

_____

_____

_____

_____

Passage 2

　　技術支援是基本的服務內容。會展中心要能提供越來越完善的技術服務。許多客戶自己設計演示軟體，要求有相應的技術支援。在會展中心有各種各樣的投影設備，一般與其他媒體結合使用。多媒體包括放像、電腦文本和構圖、數碼相機圖像轉換、在演示中增加影像效果。另一個技術方面的問題，是音響以及擴音需求。除了最小型的活動之外，都會有這方面的要求。為保證所需設備到位,場地管理方和技術人員應該要求演講者至少在活動開始一周前到場調試設備。

Your Answer

_____

_____

_____

_____

_____

_____

_____

_____

Reference Answers

A. Sentence Interpretation

1. 你有那麼多的事情要記,應該分出輕重緩急,應該注意最新的一些變化,留意給你的便條、信函、電話、留言和電子郵件等。

2. 檢查一下管理協調人員與員工的工作安排,處理所有最後的報名和變更情況。

3. 所有員工穿有特定顏色的制服,胸前掛有身份證件,易於辨認。

4. 貨物送達後,不可能你在哪裡,就在哪裡收貨。

5. 現在,活動期間的用餐流行一種主題化餐飲,這是一種美味佳餚與娛樂相結合的活動。

6. One of the frequently discussed issues in convention management is the extent to which the salesperson should be involved in the servicing process.

7. It is the exhibitor or the attendee who is receiving the service, not the convention and exhibition staff who is delivering it, whose expectations count.

8. We will empower our staff to exceed out guests' expectations and to become guest obsessed.

9. Various things will be delivered as preparations progress.

10. Exhibitions and trade fairs usually succeed because they attract enough visitors to satisfy the exhibitors and enough exhibitors to satisfy the visitors.

B. Passage Interpretation

Passage 1

　　物流業務是指計劃並統整物品、設備與人員的流動。物流業務包括票務、問詢,參觀者的接送和工作人員在展館的流動。就物流而言,一項活動的準備、開幕和運轉要求所有環節在一定的時間內準備就緒。這是一個非常複雜的過程。

每一個人和部門要通力合作並按照各自的工作要求做好準備。一旦活動開始，會展主辦方要保證萬無一失。貨物的預定與驗收一般在集中收貨區進行。從那裡，將貨物分送到指定的地點。

Technical services and support are thought to be essential. Convention and exhibition centers are expected to provide technical services that are increasingly sophisticate. Many clients will design audiovisual presentations and suggest the appropriate use of technology. At convention and exhibition centers, video projection of various kinds is available and is often used in conjunction with other media. Multimedia can include video, computer-generated text and graphics, transfer of pictures from digital cameras and the insertion of sound or video into presentations. The other frequent technical issue is that of sound and the need for sound reinforcement, in all but the smallest events. To ensure that the required equipment is available, the venue management and technical staff should request that presenters come and test their material at least a week prior to the event.

Section 2
Speaking Activities

A. Specialized Terms

Match the expressions on the left with the best Chinese equivalent on the right.

1. booth number	A. 展臺索引
2. closing date for applications	B. 人員雜費
3. one-stop services	C. 起租面積
4. Incidental expense	D. 英 / 中文招牌
5. service fee	E. 展臺號
6. bank account number	F. 現場服務
7. minimum area	G. 服務費
8. on-site services	H. 英中文對照展覽指南
9. bilingual exhibition directory	I. 一條龍服務
10. English/Chinese stand fascia	J. 報名截止期

B. Sample Conversation

Rread aloud.

Situation: Mr. Li with the Dragon Translation Service is interviewing Ding Xiao for a job as an interpreter.

Woman:　Good afternoon, Mr. Li. I 've heard from Dragon Translation Service you want to hire an interpreter. I wonder if I could have the chance to get the position.

Man:　Good afternoon. Please introduce yourself first.

Woman:　Yes, my name is Ding Xiao. I'm a native of Taipei and can speak standard Mandarin. Now I'm majoring in English in NCCU for nine years, and I also know a little French and German.

Man:　You sound just the person we need. But since you are still a student, how can you do this job full-time?

Woman:　It is our summer holiday, and I'm free for almost two months.

Man:　That's fine. But have you interpreted at trade shows before and will you be able to interpret technical terms?

Woman:　Yes. I worked as an interpreter at last year's International Toy Exposition.

Man:　That's Good. When will you be available for the job?

Woman:　Any time. Our vacation has just started and I am free already..

Man:　Ok. Would you come to Hilton Hotel at 10 a.m. Thursday morning?

Woman:　Yes, of course. See you then,

Man:　That's really reasonable. Thank you very much for the information. I have to talk this with my teammates and let you know our decision in two weeks.

Woman:　I really appreciate that. If you have any question, please do not hesitate to contact me.

Man: We will. Thanks again. Goodbye, Mr. Li.

Woman: See you , Miss Ding.

C. Functional Expressions

Read aloud and practice with your partner.

1. What is on the list of renting?

2. Is the renting cost included in the price for using the venue?

3. How much does it cost?

4. What is the price for renting one spotlight per day?

5. What should I do to hire an electrician?

6. Where should I settle the accounts?

7. Would you please the exhibition service desk?

D. Speaking Up

Render the following into English by using as many language skills learnt as possible.

1. 一張圓桌每天的租用費用是多少？

2. 充分的準備可以帶來完美的開始。

3. 我們需要租些花卉和盆景，讓我們的展臺更美觀。

4. 需要租什麼東西？

5. 請問請翻譯怎麼收費？

E. Role-play

Practice the conversations in English according to the situations.

Situation 1

Mr. Smith is the representative of a textile company, which is planning to attend a textile show. He is asking for some information about the renting of facilities at the rental desk of the exhibition center. Mrs. Li is a clerk at the rental desk and she is answering Mr. Smith's questions and providing some suggestions.

Situation 2

Two companies sponsored a volunteer effort to clean up the city's park. Two persons from the companies are discussing this event.

Situation 3

Two staff members from an exhibiting company are discussing the rental of some equipments. Please try the dialogue using your real names in pairs.

Situation 4

Rose is working at the exhibition service desk. Now she is showing an exhibitor how to rent some necessary equipments and items.

Reference Answer

A. Specialized Terms

1.E   2.J   3.I   4.B   5.G   6.K   7.C   8.F
9.H   10.D

D. Speaking Up

1. How much do you charge for renting a round table per day?

2. Good preparation makes a perfect beginning.

3. What is on the list of renting?

4. We need to rent some flowers and plants to make our stand look much better?

5. How much does it cost to hire an interpreter?

Chapter 10
Safety and Security Service
安保服務

Go over the following words and expressions before listening to the tape.

amplification			擴音器
infrared systems			紅外系統
seating layout			座位安排
overhead projector			實物投影機
shell schemes			框架式展臺
gangway			側廊
pendant mike		n.	吊式麥克風
roving mike		n.	手持麥克風
adjustable		a.	可調節的
keynote speakers			主要發言人
cordless mikes			無線麥克風
renovation		n.	裝修
drapery		n.	圍布
exterior		n.	外飾
meticulously		adv.	謹慎地

Section 1
Interpretation Activities

A. Sentence Interpretation

1. First, find out the equivalents of the following words.

sanitation staff entrance area CCTV (closed circuit TV) cameras time-recording equipment 保全代理機構 有毒，易腐蝕或易燃性化學製品或氣體 維護和保護 遙控觀察和監控	

2. Read the following to your partner for him or her to put them down in Chinese or English.

1. Safety is a major consideration in all aspects of meeting, exhibition and hotel operation.

2. CCTV cameras fall into several categories.

3. Identification systems are commonly installed in the staff entrance area, together with time-recording equipment.

4. Theft by staff and service personnel is also a matter for concern.

5. Food and beverage safety and sanitation is also essential to the success of a convention or exhibition.

6. 會議策劃者應在預定會議時建議籌備者負責危急情況的員警和保全代理機構。

7. 車輛出入口是需要安裝攝像機的關鍵地方。

8. 大樓內外區域的遙控觀察和監控是保全和管理經營中至關重要的部分。

9. 參展商應該負責自己參展品的維護和保護。我們建議照相機和其他貴重的小件物品應有人照看。

10. 未經科學展銷會安全官員批准不得使用有毒、腐蝕性或易燃的化學品或氣體。 一般地應避免危險的化學製品。

B. Passage Interpretation

1. First, find out the equivalents of the following words.

burglar and fire alarm audio and video intercom 預防措施 人員受傷，財產損壞或者法律行為 嚴格執行	

2. Read the following passages to yourself and render them into Chinese or English.

Passage 1

　　Supreme Security Systems is the largest independent, full-service electronic security provider in New Jersey. The company provides over 10,000 businesses, industrial facilities and residences with the most advanced burglar and fire alarms, closed circuit TV (CCTV) systems, access control systems and process and environmental monitoring systems, audio and video intercoms and music systems.

Your Answer

_____

_____

_____

_____

_____

_____

_____

_____

Passage 2

　　把公共安全作為首要考慮是至關重要的。應該採取適當的預防措施保證不會造成人員受傷、財產損壞或者法律行為等嚴重後果。所有展品都必須符合以下標準，保全人員也要嚴格執行這些標準。

Your Answer

_____

_____

_____

_____

_____

_____

Reference Answer

A. Sentence Interpretation

1. words

sanitation	衛生
staff entrance area	員工入口區
CCTV (closed circuit TV) cameras	閉路監控電視
time-recording equipment	打卡機
保全代理機構	security agencies
有毒、易腐蝕或易燃性化學製品或氣體	toxic, corrosive or flammable chemicals or gasses
維護和保護	maintenance and protection
遠端觀察和監控	remote observation and monitoring

2. sentences

1. 安全是會議、展覽和飯店經營中各個方面都應考慮的主要事情。

2. 閉路攝影機有好幾種類型。

3. 身份辨識系統一般都與考勤機一起安裝在員工入口處。

4. 員工和服務人員的偷竊也是要考慮的問題。

5. 食品飲料的安全與衛生也是會議或展覽成功的關鍵。

6. A meeting planner should advise the organizer of police and security agencies on risks at time of booking.

7. Vehicle entrances and exits are typical locations for cameras.

8. Remote observation and monitoring of areas inside and outside the building is an essential part of security and management operations.

9. Exhibitors are responsible for the maintenance and protection of their own exhibits during the Fair. We recommend that cameras and other expensive small items not be left unattended.

10. No toxic, corrosive or flammable chemicals or gasses are allowed unless approved by the Science Fair Safety Officer. In general, dangerous chemicals should be avoided.

B. Passage Interpretation

1. words

burglar and fire alarm	盜竊和火災警報
audio and video intercom	視聽通訊裝置
預防措施	precautions
人員受傷，財產損壞或者	personal injury, property damage, or
法律行為	legal action
嚴格執行	be rigidly enforced

2. paragraph

Passage 1

高級安全系統是紐澤西州最大的、獨立的和全面服務電子安全系統提供商。該公司為萬餘家商業、工業企業和居民客戶提供最高級的盜竊和火災警報、閉路電視系統、入口監控系統和過程與環境監控系統、視聽對講裝置以及音樂系統。

▌Passage 2

It is essential that safety to the public be a prime consideration. Suitable precautions must be taken to help ensure that serious consequences do not result in terms of personal injury, property damage, or legal action. All exhibits must conform to the following standards which will be rigidly enforced by the Safety Officer.

Section 2
Speaking Activities

A. Specialized Terms

Match the expressions on the left with the best Chinese equivalent on the right.

貴重物品	Fire prevention equipment
防火設備	Hidden property
威脅或危機評估	Valuables
隱蔽物品	Evacuation route
電腦犯罪／駭客	Hack

反入侵系統	Evaluation of threat and crisis
逃生路線	Monitor screen
監視器	Identification PLATE
微波護欄	Statutory obligations
身分牌	Anti-invasion system
法律責任	Infrared guard

B. Sample Conversation

Read aloud.

Situation: A meeting planner is checking the meeting safety and security measures with the organizer.

Planner: I'm told you've got a latest model of CCTV system. Then what kind of cameras do you use?

Organizer: Well, actually we are using several kinds of cameras, depending on the location, lens requirements and head operations.

Planner: Could you make it clear?

Organizer: Yes, Mr. Williams. We have cameras both indoor and outdoor with different angles of views.

Planner: What about lens?

Organizer: We have installed remote iris adjustment, footing and zooming ones. And for head operation, we have pans and tilt cameras.

Planner: And I think you also need to consider that positions of nearby lamps could shine into the lens and cause glare.

Organizer: You are right. We have solved this problem, and we also use silicon-vidicon cameras in parallel with infra-red beams foe night vision.

C. Functional Expressions

Read aloud and practice with your partner.

What kind of cameras do you use?

Do you provide a lockable cupboard or storage area on the stand?

Can we have a name list of the security guards?

Be sure your valuable items are attended on your stand.

We offer 24 hour security service at the venue.

Flammable and explosive items should not be left unattended.

No toxic, corrosive or flammable chemicals or gasses are allowed unless approved by the safety officer.

Make it sure that heat sources must not be used near combustible materials.

Excuse me, Sir. We are the security officers of the venue. Can we have a look of your exhibits?

Excuse me, officer. One of our exhibits is missing. Can you help us to find it?

D. Speaking Up

Translate the following sentences into English by using as

many language skills learnt as possible.

1. 請給我們一份保全人員的清單。

2. 我們提供 24 小時現場保全服務。

3. 易燃易爆物品須有專人保管。

4. 確保在易燃物品遠離熱源。

5. 我們是現場保全。請讓我們檢查一下您的展品。

E. Role-play

Practice the conversations in English according to the situations.

Situation 1

Role A: You're an exhibitor who is planning to exhibit the latest products of your company at the 21st International Jewelry Exhibition that will be hosted by Shanghai New Century Exhibition Center. You are calling the center to consult the Security facilities to ensure your safety concerns about your exhibits. Your name is Peter Johnson.

Role B: You are a receptionist at Shanghai New Century Exhibition Center. Try to give Mr. Peter satisfactory answers to sooth his worries.

Situation 2

Role A: You are the Meeting organizer of Grand Hotel. The annual meeting Canada Association of Stockers will be held in your hotel. Mr. David Hansen is now at your hotel to have an inspection. You are accompanying him. Answer his questions about safety and security concerns.

Role B: You are Mr. David Hansen, the meeting planner of Canada Association of Stockers. You are inspecting the meeting hotel so as to make sure about the security faculties to guarantee the success of the meeting. You concerns Include CCTV, the emergency exits and other details.

Reference Answer

A. Specialized Terms

1.C　2.A　3.F　4.B　5.E　6.J　7.D　8.G
9.D　10.H　11.I

D. Speaking Up

1. Can we have a name list of the security guards?

2. We offer 24 hour security service at the venue.

3. Flammable and explosive items should not be left unattended.

4. Make it sure that heat sources must not be used near combustible materials.

5. We are the security officers of the venue. Can we have a look of your exhibits?

Chapter 11

Helping with Post-Conference Logistics 會後物流服務

Go over the following words and expressions before listening to the tape.

mode of shipping		運輸方式
delivery		發貨 / 交貨
bulky	a.	大宗的
risk of theft		盜險
ocean freight		海洋運輸
inventory	n.	庫存 / 存貨
transit	n.	轉運
airport shuttle bus		機場接駁車
CIP (cost' insurance and freight) price		到岸價
A.R. (all risks)		綜合險
F.P.A (free of particular average)		平安險
W.P.A (with particular average)		水漬險
B/L (bill of lading)		提單
the assured		保險商
avert	v.	避免
carrier	n.	承運人
bailee	n.	受託人
claim	v.	索賠
defective	a.	受損的
container	n.	集裝箱

Section 1
Interpretation Activities

A. Sentence Interpretation

1. First, find out the equivalents of the following words.

1. innovation		7. 經裝修一新	
2. attendance		8. 影像設備	
3. distraction		9. 省去 ...... 的麻煩	
4. keynoter		10. 滿足要求	
5. attendee		11. 會議套餐	
6. limo (limousin)			

2. Read the following to your partner for him or her to put them down in Chinese or English.

1. Where you want to go will determine what method to get there. For example, if you want to go downtown, you may have a few options, like bicycle, taxi, limo, or bus.

2. If a reservation is needed, first you need to check availability.

3. Delivery of the ticket is usually quick: it is even faster to book an e-ticket.

4. Business class passengers may also choose the maglev to the airport, where they will board their airplane.

5. Drop off, pickup, and transfers can all cause problems if the language or transportation systems are very different than

those the passenger has at their home.

6. 一般來說，有三種主要的交通方式，即地面交通、軌道和航空。

7. 國際聯合運輸（multimodal transport）是指兩國間根據多式聯運合約，採用至少兩種運輸方式，將貨物從發貨地運往目的地。

8. 出口貨物常常採用集裝箱運輸。集裝箱運輸對聯合運輸尤其適合。

9. 在交通方面，有很多問題發生在下客、搭載和轉乘時。

10. 全程運輸中當貨物不轉運，直接從裝貨港運至目的港，承運人或其代理就簽發給托運人（shipper）一張直運提單。

B. Passage Interpretation

1. First, find out the equivalents of the following words.

methods of delivery		東西向高架	
cargo space		南北向高架	
mark		輕軌	
waybill			
consignment			
dispatch			

2. Read the following passages to yourself and render them into Chinese or English.

Passage 1

Normally, the bill of lading contains detailed provisions about the methods of delivery and the cessation of the carrier's liability. Regardless of the kind of carrier to be used, the carrier will issue a "booking contract", reserving space for the cargo on a specified vessel. We shall be glad to know the time of transit and frequency of sailing, and whether cargo space must be reserved; if so, please send us the necessary application forms. The goods have been packed and marked exactly as directed so that they may be shipped as soon as possible. A waybill, giving full particulars, will be sent to you as soon as the consignment is ready for dispatch by Eastern Airlines.

Your Answer

_____

_____

_____

_____

_____

_____

_____

Reference Answer

A. Sentence Interpretation

1. words

1. innovation	創新
2. attendance	參加會議的人數
3. distraction	干擾物
4. keynoter	主要發言人
5. attendee	與會者
6. limo (limousin)	豪華轎車
7. 經裝修一新	completely renovated
8. 影像設備	audiovisual equipment
9. 省去 …… 的麻煩	save the trouble
10. 滿足要求	meet one's demand
11. 會議套餐	meeting package

2. sentences

1. 你的目的地將決定你選擇什麼樣的交通工具。比方說，如果你要想去市中心，你可能有好幾種選擇，如腳踏車、計程車、豪華轎車和公車。

2. 如果需要預訂，你首先要查票務資訊，確認是否有票。

3. 送票通常很快，如果預定的是電子票，速度更快。

4. 商務艙的乘客也可能選擇搭乘磁浮列車去機場。

5. 如果乘客語言不通且又完全不熟悉當地交通系統，那麼他們在下車、搭載和轉乘時都可能碰到麻煩。

6. In general, there are three main kinds of transportation, ground, rail and air.

7. International multimodal transport means the conveyance of cargo between two countries by at least two models of transport from the place of dispatch to that of destination on the basis of a multimodal transport contract.

8. The transportation of export goods is frequently carried out in containers, which are particularly suitable for multimodal transport.

9. One difficult part where a lot of problems happen in transportation is in drop, pickup and transfers.

10. Direct bill of lading is issued by the carrier or his agent to the shipper when the Goods are transported directly from the port of loading to that of destination without transshipment during the whole voyage.

B. Passage Interpretation

1. words

methods of delivery	遞交方式
cargo space	貨艙
mark	標記
waybill	運貨單
consignment	委託
dispatch	派發，派遣
東西向高架	East-west Elevated Highway

南北向高架	South-north Elevated Highway
輕軌	Light rail

2. paragraph

▌ Passage 1

　　通常，提單包含交貨方式、承運人責任截止期等資訊。不論採取何種運輸方式，承運人都需要簽訂一份「訂艙合約」，預訂好指定貨船上的艙位。請告知運輸時間有多長、有多少航次、貨艙是否需要預定。如需要預訂，請將訂艙表寄來。貨物已嚴格按照要求包裝妥當，刷好標記，以便儘快運出。貨物備妥，東方航空公司發運時，我們會把一份載明明細的空運單寄給你們。

Section 2
Speaking Activities

A. Specialized Terms

Match the expressions on the left with the best Chinese equivalent on the right.

1. shipping specialist 　　＿＿＿＿＿A. 運費表

2. forwarding agent 　　＿＿＿＿＿B. 郵資

3. destination   _____C. 專業輸送

4. postage   _____D. 損失

5. tariff   _____E. 目的地

6. damage   _____F. 總帳單

7. price catalogue   _____G. 價格表

8. freight rate   _____H. 運輸代理

9. dispatch   _____I. 發送

10. master account   _____J. 運輸費

B. Sample Conversation

Read aloud.

Situation: Mr. Hilton, meeting planner, is in a hurry on his way to the convention service manager's office. He is wondering if the convention service manager (CSM) could help find him a express delivery company to handle the bulky meeting stuff.

CSM: Good morning Mr. Hilton. Is there anything I can do for you?

Hilton: I'm looking for a delivery company. You know, the conference has come to a successful close. And there stuffs to be sent back home. Can you suggest a company to take care of them?

CSM: Yes. We have in-house delivery service right here. We are shipping specialists and can provide you excellent service.

Hilton:　Oh, that'll be wonderful. We really appreciate your service in the past. And I have trust in your staff.

CSM:　Thank you, Mr. Hilton. May I ask what kind of materials you'd like to deliver?

Hilton:　We have name signs of the attendees that we want to reuse at next conference, some meeting documents, and some other stuff.

CSM: That's quite a lot. But don't worry. Our crew can handle them professionally and promptly. We are faster than airlines. Where do you want them?

Hilton:　To San Francisco. Here is our address.

CSM:　I see. Then how quickly do you need them delivered?

Hilton:　Is it possible that our headquarters will receive them in two days?

CSM:　It depends. If the packages are ready by now, it will take less time for our employees to move. Have you packed them in advance?

Hilton:　No, we haven't. I wonder if you could help.

CSM:　No problem. We also have professional packing crew and adequate packing facilities. But it will Incur extra charge for the packing.

Hilton:　You may charge it and the freight rates to our master account. What are the rates for the packing and the delivery service?

CSM:　Here's the price tag, sir. Please take a look at it. As you can see, our prices are quite competitive in the city.

Hilton: Well, sure reasonable. I need a guarantee that the package will be there.

CSM: We do guarantee if you agree to the terms of delivery.

Hilton: Ok. I don't see there is any problem.

CSM: Now please sign your name on the contract here, and here, the names of the objects to be delivered. We'll send our people up to handle the packing right away.

C. Functional Expressions

Read aloud and practice with your partner.

Common questions for convention express delivery or shipment

What kind of material you'd like to deliver?

Where do you want them?

How soon do you want them to reach the destination?

How quickly do you need them delivered?

Do you agree with the payment terms?

May I suggest express delivery be made?

Would you please take a look at the tariff?

Could you make a list of further instructions about shipment of convention materials?

May I know when we could expect the delivery?

Do you guarantee that the packet will be there on time?

Could you deliver the packet immediately?

Can't you make the delivery a little earlier?

What's the earliest possible date then?

What are the rates of the packeting and the delivery service?

D. Speaking Up

Understand the speaker's intention, and then fill in the blanks.

1. ——_____.
   ——The earliest time of delivery is 4 days form now.

   （用意：詢問收貨日期）

2. ——_____?
   ——No problem. We can deliver the packet in an hour to meet your requirement.

   （用意：要求儘快起運）

3. ——_____?
   ——This kind of packeting costs more.

   （用意：詢問包裝費用）

4. ——We want these materials to reach our destination by Christmas.

   ——_____.

   （用意：建議快遞服務）

5. ——_____?
   ——We enforce the packets with iron straps.

   （用意：詢問包裝方式）

E. Role-play

Practice the conversation in English.

A: 希爾頓先生，你能確定所有被租用的設備都列在物品清單上了嗎？

B: 讓我看看，兩臺錄音設備，一臺投影機，三個麥克風。是的，全齊了。

A: 會議一結束，供應商就會馬上把設備運走嗎？

B: 我恐怕到時他們不會馬上來。你能安全保管這些物品並把他們交還給供應商嗎？

A: 當然可以，我們會把這些設備保護好的。

B: 那些標識牌怎麼辦？下次會議我們還會用到。

A: 這個我們也想到了。我們的服務員會收集所有的標識牌，然後交還給你們。

B: 那太好了，我真的很感謝你們的細心幫助。運輸費用怎麼算？

A: 220 元。

B: 好的，把費用記在總帳單上。

A: 我們會照辦的。

Refernece Answer

A. Specialized Terms

1.C　　2.H　　3.E　　4.B　　5.A　　6.D　　7.G　　8.J
9.I　　10.F

D. Speaking Up

1. When can the delivery be made?

2. Can you make the deliver as soon as possible?

3. What do you charge for the packeting?

4. We would suggest the express delivery service.

5. How do you packet these boxes?

Chapter 12
Opening and Reception 開幕與酒會

Go over and expressions the following words.

boost		v.	推進，提高
visibility		n.	能見度
infrastructure		n.	基礎結構，基礎設施
the International Bureau of Exposition(IBE)			國際博覽局
refreshment		n.	點心
sales representative			銷售代表
R&D (research and development)			研發
call filter			電話過濾
thriving		a	繁榮的
highlight		v.	突出，強調

Section 1
Interpretation Activities

A. Sentence Interpretation

1. First, find out the equivalents of the following words.

1. booth	
2. function book entries	
3. entrée	
4. specialty or theme restaurant	
5. appetizer	
6. spicy	

7. tart	
8. 畫架	
9. 分時預訂	
10. 交錯預訂	
11. 點菜單	
12. 單獨定價	
13. 套餐，公司餐	
14. 固定價格	

2. Read the following to your partner for him or her to put them down in Chinese or English.

1. The current trend toward light cuisine is continued at most banquet luncheons. Fish and chicken are the entrées of choice with many meeting planners. Formal luncheons offering heavy sauces, rich desserts, and alcoholic beverages spell trouble to most planners and have therefore declined in popularity.

2. Easels, chart boards, movie screens, tables for projectors, and extension cords are included in function room rental rates while computers for PowerPoint presentations, VCRs, slide projectors, overhead projectors are charged separately.

3. The use of reservation is a convenience and service to guests as well as a tool that helps staff members recognize guests by name, guarantee speed and quality of service, and promote production efficiency.

4. There are two basic types of reservation systems—interval reservations and staggered reservations. The interval

reservations system offers seating at specific intervals during the meal period while the staggered reservations system staggers seating during the entire meal period and reservations can be made for any time that tables are available during the meal period.

5. An a la carte menu is a menu which offers choices in each course and in which each item is individually priced and charged for. A table d'hote menu offers some (usually limited) choices and is charged at a fixed price for the whole menu.

6. 預訂員填寫訂單時應該獲取以下資訊：以誰的名義預訂、名字的正確寫法、預訂的時間、日期、人數、需要有煙還是無煙區、一般餐桌還是包廂、有無特殊要求，以及客人的電話號碼。

7. 餐飲任務登記一般包括團名、客戶姓名、頭銜和電話號碼；預計出席人數；項目名稱以及活動類型。

8. 對於多數會議型飯店來說，宴會的收入僅次於客房。

9. 主菜通常最先點。主菜包括牛肉、豬肉、魚和沙拉（涼拌菜）等。許多特色餐館或主題餐館提供的主菜種類相對較少，這樣可以最大程度地減少內部烹調和服務問題。

10. 開胃菜包括水果汁或番茄汁、乳酪、水果和海鮮類。開胃菜是就餐前用來開胃的，因此他們的量一般較少，通常帶辛辣味或酸味，口感較好。

B. Passage Interpretation

1. First, find out the equivalents of the following words.

1. specialty menu		9. 生的 / 地	
2. cereal		10. 半成品的	
3.waffle		11. 領班	
4. watchword		12. 助理	
5. take-out		13. 餐館打雜工	
6. pasta dish		14. 副領班	
7. lasagna		15. 服務站	
8. linguine		16. 廚師	

2. Read the following passages to yourself and render them into Chinese or English.

Passage 1

Cart Service is called "French Service" in the United States and in Germany; yet in France, Cart Service is referred to as "Russian Service". The food is brought to the guests' table in either a raw state or a semi-prepared state and finished in front of the guests in the dining room on a cart. The final food preparation is performed by the chef de rang, and he/she is assisted by a commis de rang. Although the chef de rang has been called a captain or a waiter, he/she performs some of the tasks performed by a waiter and some of the tasks a captain usually performs. The commis de rang is referred to as a bus boy but performs many more service-related functions than is usually given a bus boy. A demichef de rang is a commis de rang who has recently been promoted and is given a small station as well as the assistance of a commis.

The chef de rang and the commis work together as a team in a station of approximately twenty guests. The chef de rang prepares the food and places the food on the plates, while the commis actually serves the guest. Each of these two individuals must be highly skilled, sInce the chef de rang is performing many of the functions in the dining room that the cook performs in the kitchen.

Your Answer

_____

_____

_____

_____

_____

_____

_____

_____

Passage 2

　　菜單的定價方式有三種，他們是套餐價、單點價以及單點和套餐相結合的定價方式。套餐菜單給整餐提供一個價格。單點菜單上,每道菜、每種飲料都列出來單獨定價。

　　三種基本的菜單為早餐、午餐和晚餐。特色菜單是為了吸引特定的客戶群體或滿足特定的市場需求。

　　典型的早餐菜單提供水果、果汁、蛋類、穀物、薄煎餅、華夫餅以及像燻肉、香腸一類供早餐用的肉食。早餐功能表上的品種要遵循簡單、快捷和價廉的原則。

　　午餐客人通常比較匆忙,午餐菜單以三明治、湯和沙拉為主,這些菜製作起來相對簡單快捷。午餐菜單上的菜通常比晚餐清淡,不如晚餐那麼精緻。

　　對於大多數人來說晚餐是一天中的正餐。典型的晚餐主菜有牛排、烤肉、雞肉、海鮮以及像千層麵和寬麵條一類的義大利麵點。葡萄酒、雞尾酒和外地風味甜點更有可能出現在晚餐菜單上而不是午餐菜單上。

　　一般的特色菜單包括兒童餐單、老人菜單、含酒精類飲料菜單、甜點菜單、房內用膳菜單、外賣菜單、宴會菜單和民族特色菜單。

Your Answer

_____

_____

_____

_____

_____

Reference Answers

A. Sentence Interpretation

1. words

1. booth	包廂
2. function book entries	餐飲任務登記
3. entrée	主菜
4. specialty or theme restaurant	特色或主題餐館
5. appetizer	開胃菜
6. spicy	辛辣的
7. tart	酸的
8. 畫架	easel
9. 分時預訂	interval reservations
10. 交錯預訂	staggered reservations
11. 點菜單	a la carte menu
12. 單獨定價	be individually priced
13. 套餐，公司餐	table d'hote menu
14. 固定價格	fixed price

2. sentences

1. 目前多數午餐宴請趨向於選用清淡的飲食。許多會議策劃者選擇魚和雞肉作為主食。正式的午餐提供重口味的醬汁、豐富的甜點和酒精飲料，這種午餐給多數會議策劃者招惹麻煩，已經越來越不受歡迎。

2. 功能廳（宴會廳）的租賃價格中包括畫架、告示板、布幕、投影機和接線，而 PPT 演示用的電腦以及錄影機、幻燈機、投影機則需單獨付費。

3. 預訂一方面給客人提供方便，另一方面可以使員工知道客人的姓名、保證服務的速度和品質，提高烹調效率。

4. 基本的餐飲預訂系統有兩種─分時預訂和交錯預訂。分時預訂給客人提供特定的用餐時間，而交錯預訂則指給客人交錯安排座位，只要在整個用餐時間有空桌就可預訂。

5. 零點菜單是指可以選擇每道菜並且每道菜單獨定價和收費的菜單。套餐菜單則提供較為有限的幾種選擇，而且整個菜單通常有固定的定價。

6. Reservation-takers should obtain the following information from callers: the correct spelling of the name the reservation will be under, the date and time of the reservation, the number in the party, whether a smoking or non-smoking section is preferred, whether the guests want a table or a booth, special instructions, and the guest's phone number.

7. Function book entries typically include the group's name; the client's name, title, and phone number; the estimated attendance; the name of the event; and the type of event.

8. For most convention hotels, banquet functions are second only to the sale of guestrooms in generating revenue.

9. Entrées are usually selected first. They include beef, pork, fish, entrée salad, etc. Many specialty or theme restaurants offer relatively few entrées. This minimizes many in-house production and serving problems.

10. Appetizers include fruit or tomato juice, cheese, fruit, and seafood items. Appetizers are supposed to enliven the appetite before dinner, so they are generally small in size and spicy or pleasantly biting or tart.

B. Passage Interpretation

1. First, find out the equivalents of the following words.

1. specialty menu	特色菜單	9. 生的 / 地	in a raw state
2. cereal	穀物	10. 半成品的	semi-prepared
3. waffle	華夫餅	11. 領班	chef de rang
4. watchword	口號，格言	12. 助理	commis de rang
5. take-out	外賣	13. 餐館打雜工	bus boy
6. pasta dish	義大利麵點	14. 副領班	demi chef de rang
7. lasagna	千層麵	15. 服務站	station
8. linguine	扁麵條	16. 廚師	cook

2. paragraph

Passage 1

在美國和德國，餐車服務被叫作法式服務;但是在法國，這種服務指的是俄式服務。食物在生的或者是半成品狀態下拿到客人的桌上，並且在餐廳的餐車上當著客人的面製作成成品。成品食物由領班準備，一般會有一個助理協助他。雖然領班一直被稱作組長或服務員，他／她既要承擔服務員的工作又要做領班的工作。助理指跑菜員，但他要比一般的跑菜員履行更多與服務相關的職責。副領班是新近被提拔的助理，他負責一個小型服務站，並有助理來協助他。

領班和助理組成一組，他們的服務站大約有 20 個客人。領班準備食物、給食物裝盤，真正給客人上菜的是助理。領班要在餐廳裡完成廚師在廚房完成的許多工作，這樣，他們每個人就必須有精湛的手藝。

Passage 2

The three types of menu pricing styles are table d'hote, a la carte, and combination table d'hote/ a la carte. A table d'hote menu offers a complete meal for one price. With an a la carte menu, food and beverage items are listed and priced separately.

Three basic types of menus are breakfast, lunch, and dinner menus. Specialty menus appeal to a specific guest group or meet a specific marketing need.

Breakfast menus typically offer fruits, juices, eggs, cereals, pancakes, waffles, and breakfast meats like bacon and sausage. The watchwords for breakfast menu items are "simple", "fast", and "inexpensive".

Since lunch guests are usually in a hurry, lunch menus must feature menu items that are relatively easy and quick to make, such as sandwiches, soups, and salads. Lunch menu items are usually lighter and less elaborate than dinner menu items.

Dinner is the main meal of the day for most people. Steaks, roasts, chicken, seafood, and pasta dishes like lasagna and linguine are typical dinner entrées. Wines, cocktails, and exotic desserts are more likely to be on a dinner menu than on a lunch menu.

Common specialty menus Include children's, senior citizens', alcoholic beverage, dessert, room service, take-out, banquet, and ethnic.

Section 2
Speaking Activities

A. Specialized Terms

Match the expressions on the left with the best Chinese equivalent on the right.

1. a la carte	A. 開瓶費
2. cash bar	B. 餐飲零點
3. continental breakfast	C. 單獨付費酒吧
4. corkage	D. 法式服務
5. covers/ head count	E. 歐陸式早餐
6. French service	F. 客人人數
7. guarantee	G. 最多人數
8. luncheon	H. 主題晚會
9. plated buffet	I. 裝盤式自助餐
10. refreshment break	J. 包餐，公司餐
11. table d'hote	K. 早中飯
12. theme party	L. 茶點時間

B. Sample Conversation

Listen and read aloud.

Situation 1: A reservationist is receiving a telephone call from the president of "Green Cities", who wants to book a banquet for Friday.

Booking a Reception

Staff: Good morning. New International Conference and Exhibition Center. How may I help you?

Customer: Good morning. This is Brown, President of "Green Cities". I'd like to reserve a banquet for Friday.

Staff: What time would you like it?

Customer: **At 7:00.**

Staff: How Many in your party?

Customer: **80.**

Staff: Well, our Lotus Hall will do.

Customer: Could we take up the menu choice now?

Staff: **Sure.**

Customer: As for the menu choice, we'd like the routine entrée and chef's choice for the banquet.

Staff: How would you like the banquet to be served?

Customer: French service. By the way, can you preset the furniture for the banquet before 6:30 p.m.?

Staff: Sure. We will take care of it.

Customer: What is the minimum you charge for each attendee?

Staff: 1320 NT dollars per person, premium brands excluded.

Customer: How are call brands charged?

Staff: Usually by the bottle, but we can also charge by the drink.

Customer: I prefer the latter. Is there any service charge for it?

Staff: Yes. There will also be other charges, such as corkage if drinks are brought from outside.

Customer: Well, in this case, house brands would be fine.

Staff: OK, Mr. Brown.

Customer: May I put the charges on to the master account?

Staff: Yes. Anything else I can do for you?

Customer: That's all.

C. Sample Closing and Thank-you Speech

Read aloud.

Situation 2: Mr. Brown is President of the symposium, which is coming to a close. He is now holding a dinner party for the attendees and making a closing and thank-you speech.

Mr. Vice President,

Our American friends,

My colleagues,

Ladies and gentlemen,

On behalf of all the members of mission, I would like to express our sIncere thanks to you for inviting us to such a marvelous dinner party.

We really enjoyed the delicious food and excellent wine. Also, the music was perfect. I enjoyed meeting and talking to you, and sharing the time together. As we say, well begin is half done. I hope we will be able to maintain this Good relationship and make next year another great one.

Thank you again for the wonderful part, we had a great time.

In closing, I would like to invite you to join me in a toast.

To the health of Mr. Vice President.

To the health of our American friends.

To the health of my colleagues.

And to all the ladies and gentlemen present here.

Cheers!

D. Functional Expressions

Read aloud and practice with your partner.
Receiving a reservation call

> Good morning. Chinese Restaurant. Reservations. How may I help you?
>
> Good afternoon. Western Restaurant. What can I do for you?

Time

> When would you like your table, sir?
>
> How many people are there in your party, sir?
>
> Could you please tell me the number of diners, sir?
>
> Guest's name and telephone
>
> May I have your name and telephone number, sir?
>
> Could you please tell me your name and telephone number, sir?
>
> Your name and telephone number, please?
>
> Under whose name, please?

Requirements

> Any other requirements?
>
> Anything special, please?

Confirmation

> So, it's Mr. White, a table for five at 6:30 p.m. this evening. Am I right?
>
> A table near the window for Mr. White for 3 at 12:00. Am I

right?

A table for 3 this evening under the name of Mr. White. Will that be all right?

How to summarize a conference

We have come to the end of the...

I wish I could give you a meaningful summary of...

It is quite impossible for me to summarize the proceedings, but I would like to mention...

How to express thanks

I would like to thank...

I wish to thank...

On behalf of..., I wish to express our sincere gratitude to...

Thank you again for...

How to announce the next conference or congress

It is a privilege for me to announce that the next...to be held in...

I now have the duty and the honor to declare the...officially closed.

Now I declare the conference closed.

How to propose a toast

In closing, I would like to invite you to join me in a toast.

Let's drink a toast to...

Let me propose a toast to the health of...

To..., cheers!

E. Speaking Up

Render the following into English by using as many language skills learnt as possible.

1. 大會已近尾聲，組委會的全體成員由衷感謝所有與會者的通力合作。

2. 雖然我難以把大會上的每一件事情都加以總結，但是我想把一些重點提一下。

3. 感謝主席、發言者以及所有與會者所作的貢獻。

4. 我代表組委會的所有成員，向你們表示真誠的感謝，是你們使這次研討會如此成功。

5. 現在，我榮幸地宣布大會正式閉幕。

6. 在結束之際，我想邀請各位一起舉杯祝酒。為在場的所有女士們、先生們，乾杯！

F. Role-play

Render the following into English by using as many language skills learnt as possible

A headwaiter is receiving a telephone call from a local customer to book a none-smoking table for a party of six for tonight.

Situation 2

You are the emcee of a conference. Please extend an address on the closing ceremony. Cover the following points when delivering the speech.

1. Summarizing the congress briefly
2. Expressing thanks to all the participants for their contributions
3. Announcing the next congress will be held in 2007
4. Announcing the conference closed

Situation 3

You are the president for a seminar. Now you are holding a farewell party. Please extend a closing speech and propose a toast. Cover the following points when delivering the speech.

1. Summarizing the four-day seminar, which has greatly benefited all the participants
2. Best wishes to all the participants
3. Proposing a toast

Reference Answer

A. Specialized Terms

1-b　2-c　3-e　4-a　5-f　6-d　7-g　8-k
9-i　10-l　11-j　12-h

E. Speaking Up

1. We have come to the end of the Congress. The members of our Organizing Committee are deeply grateful for the hearty cooperation of all participants.

2. It is quite impossible for me to summarize the proceedings, but I would like to mention some of the principal points that have emerged from some of the papers.

3. I wish to thank all the chairmen, speakers and other participants for their valuable contributions.

4. On behalf of all the members of our organizing committee, I wish to express our sIncere gratitude to all of you who have made the seminar such a success.

5. I now have the honor to declare the congress officially closed.

6. In closing, I would like to invite you to join me in a toast. To all the ladies and gentlemen present here, cheers!

Chapter13
Attending the Event 參加展會

Go over and expressions the following words.

BRT (bus rapid transit)			專用公交系統
congestion		n.	交通阻塞
optimize		v.	優化
integrate		v.	整合
commuter		n.	通勤者，每日往返上班者
port of discharge			卸貨港
airport representative			機場代表
promptly		ad.	立即
liability		n.	責任

Section 1
Interpretation Activities

A. Sentence Interpretation

1. Read the following to your partner for him or her to put them down in Chinese or English.

1. 展會主辦方的服務對象有兩種：一個是參展商，一個是參觀者，他們參加展會的目的各不相同。

2. 現在有越來越多的展會由會展專業人士組織，但是出於經濟原因還是有很多的展會是由機構自行組織的。

3. 大多數的資深人士傾向認為在什麼樣的場所舉辦展會比在什麼地區舉辦更重要。

4. 酒店的標準價稱作原價，但是商務客人很少按原價付款。

5. 餐飲設施與服務是商務旅遊活動取得成功的必要的前提條件。

6. In many countries, where there is an accommodation classification system, there may seem to be little relationship between quality and the official grade.

7. Organizers should ensure that they allow a margin of error so that if delays occur the event schedule will not be disrupted.

8. The informal networking is often the most part of the event, and organizers should plan opportunities for it to take place.

9. The well-established event attracts large numbers of trade and public visitors because it uses a highly professional venue with excellent facilities for both exhibitors and visitors.

10. The organizer should have a clear idea of what the ideal venue would be for their event, together with a checklist of criteria to test any venue against.

B. Passage Interpretation

1. First, find out the equivalents of the following words.

refunds space assignment Cancellations lease terminated defaulted rebate written authorization	

| 官方指定承運商
參展指南
安裝與拆卸
承諾遵守
進場與出場
消防規定
非易燃品 | |

2. Read the following passages to yourself and render them into Chinese or English.

Passage 1

Payments and refunds: The balance of the space rental charge is due and payable on or before Nov. 1, 2009. Applications received without payments will not be processed nor will space assignment be made. Cancellations received before Nov.1, 2009 will receive a refund of money paid, less 20% of the value of the original booth order. All requests for refund must be received in writing. NO REFUNDS WILL BE MADE AFTER Nov.1, 2009.

Show management: If the exhibition is not held for any reason, the rental and lease of space to the exhibitor shall be terminated. In such case, the exhibitor will get the full refund of the amount of already-paid-for spaces.

The organizer has the right to use space without payment by Nov. 1 to suit its own convenience, including selling the space to another exhibitor, without any rebate or allowance to the defaulted exhibitor. Each exhibitor must apply for his own space and no exhibitor will be permitted to assign any part of his space to another firm without written authorization from show management.

Your Answer

_____

_____

_____

_____

_____

_____

_____

_____

Passage 2

運輸須知

運輸必須有官方指定承運商裝運。承運商位址可參看《參展指南》。

展品的安裝與拆卸：所有展品必須在 2009 年 11 月 21 日展會開幕兩小時前安裝完畢。在 2009 年 11 月 23 日展會結束前，不得拆卸展品。參展商承諾遵守展會管理者關於進場與出場的規定。

消防規定：每個展位所展示的物品必須是非易燃品。參展商必須承諾遵守所有消防規定。

參展商服務指南：關於展位色彩選擇，展位空間設計，展攤設施等資訊，參展商應該詳細閱讀《參展商服務指南》。《參展商服務指南》一般於展會舉辦前 60 天發至參展商手中，或者在展位費用付清後獲得。

Your Answer

_____

_____

_____

_____

_____

_____

_____

_____

Reference Answers

A .Sentence Interpretation

1. words

1. An exhibition organizer usually has two audiences, namely exhibitors and visitors, each with different desires.

2. There is clearly a trend towards the use of professional organizers but many organizations still prefer in-house organizations largely for financial reasons.

3. Most respected commentators appear to suggest that the specific building or buildings where the event will take place should take precedence over the geographical location.

4. Standard prices in hotels are called the rack rate but very few business clients will pay this price.

5. Food and beverage is an essential prerequisite for successful business tourism events.

6. 許多國家都有旅館等級分類標準,但是這些等級分類常常與品質好壞沒什麼關係。

7. 籌備者務必要留有餘地,萬一遲延,也不會影響整個展會的排程。

8. 非正式的交流是展會的主要活動,籌備者應該為此提供方便。

9. 這個著名的展覽會吸引了大量的業內人士和一般公眾,展會的場所非常專業化,設施精良,能夠同時滿足參展商和參觀者的需要。

10. 籌備者對展會舉辦地的要求要十分明確，對每一個舉辦地按照詳細標準來進行評價。

B. Passage Interpretation

1. words

refunds	退款
space assignment	展位分配
cancellations	取消預訂
lease	租約，租期
terminated	終止
defaulted	未履約
rebate	補償
written authorization	書面同意
官方指定承運商	official drayage contractor
參展指南	Exhibitor Manual
安裝與拆卸	Exhibit installation and dismantling
承諾遵守	agree to abide by
進場與出場	move-in/move-out
消防規定	Fire regulations
非易燃品	flame retardant

2. paragraph

▌Passage 1

付款與退款

展位租借費請於 2009 年 11 月 1 日前付清。未按時付款的申請不予受理，不予租借展位。2009 年 11 月 1 日前取消預訂，已付款者可獲得原展位費 80% 的退款。所有退款申請須以書面形式遞交。2009 年 11 月 1 日後不予退款。

展會管理

如果展會不能舉行，展位租借合約終止。參展商將獲得已付展位租借費的全額退款。

主辦方對 11 月 1 日前未付費的展位享有自由處置權，包括可以將展位賣於別家參展商，未履約參展商不得進行抗辯或提出補償請求。參展商必須自己申請展位，不得未經展會管理者書面同意而私自將展位任一部份劃作其他參展商使用。

Passage 2

Shipping instructions: Shipments should be sent to the official drayage contractor. The address will be provided in the Exhibitor Manual.

Exhibit installation and dismantling: All exhibits must be completed and in place two hours prior to the opening of the exposition at on Nov.21, 2009. No exhibitor may commence the dismantling of his exhibit until the show closes on Nov. 23, 2009. Exhibitors agree to comply with the move-in/move-out schedule provided by show management.

Fire regulations: All materials used as display items in individual booths must be flame retardant. Exhibitors must agree to abide by all applicable rules and regulations of the City Fire Code.

Exhibitor's information and service manual: To develop your booth color scheme, layout, furniture requirements, etc., exhibitors should read the Exhibitor's Service MANUAL. This information will be in your hands 60 days prior to the exposition, or after payment for space has been made.

Section 2
Speaking Activities

A. Specialized Terms

Match the expressions on the left with the best Chinese equivalent on the right.

Part 1

1. non-stop flight

A. 不定期客票

2. EVA Air

B. 會議接龍

3. charter flight

C. 定期客票

4. back to back

D. 停車場服務員

5. taxi dispatcher   e. 揚招計程車

6. open ticket   f. 中途不停站的直達航班

7. OK ticket   g. 長榮航空

8. parking attendant   h. 包機飛行

9. limousine   i. 計程車調度

10. to hail a taxicab   j. (機場、車站) 接送旅客的交通車

Part 2

1. first class   A. 經濟艙

2. business class   B. 商務級艙位

3. economy class   C. 國家航空公司

4. upgrade   D. 常客

5. round trip   e. 登機證

6. charter flight   f. 艙壁座

7. coach   g. 頭等艙

8. boarding pass   h. 普通座位

9. frequent flyer   i. 往返旅行

10. flag carrier   j. 提高級別

11. bulk head   k. 貨運代理公司

12. freight forwarder   l. 包機飛行

B. Sample Conversation

Listen and read aloud.

Situation: An exhibitor telephones the Event Manager to ask him to book flight tickets for her.

Manager: Can I help the next person in line please?

Exhibitor: I'd like to get a flight to New York on April 18th and return on the 21st.

Manager: May I know your name and room number, please?

Exhibitor: Louis Fortell, Room 1108.

Manager: How Many traveling in your party, sir?

Exhibitor: **Just one.**

Manager: There are several flights to New York. When would you like to leave?

Exhibitor: Let's see. I'd like to catch an early flight out and return in the evening on the 21st.

Manager: All right. A flight leaves Taipei at 6:00 a.m. arriving in New York at 20:45. Is that too early?

Exhibitor: No, that's fine. And what about the return?

Manager: An 6:00 a.m. flight arrives back in Taipei at 10:45 p.m. How does that sound to you?

Exhibitor: Sounds Good.

Manager: Okay, I'll check that for you with the airport booking office.

Exhibitor: When can I get the tickets?

Manager: Please come again at 4:00 p.m. this afternoon, and we'll let you know if the tickets are available.

Exhibitor: Okay, thanks for your help.

C. Functional Expressions

Read aloud and practice with your partner.
Getting ticket booking information

How many traveling in your party, sir?

What airline would you prefer?

When would you like to leave?

How about the return?

Giving flight information

A flight leaves Taipei at 6:00 a.m. arriving in New York at 20:45. Is that too early?

An 6:00 a.m. flight arrives back in Taipei at 10:45 p.m. How does that sound to you?

Giving ticket information

I'll check that for you with the airport booking office.

Please come again at 4:00 p.m. this afternoon, and we'll let you know if the tickets are available.

D. Speaking Up

Render the following into English by using as many language skills learnt as possible.

A: 國際旅行社。我可以怎麼幫你呢？

B: 我想了解從上海飛往紐約的航班資訊。

A: 請問你的出發時間有什麼安排？

199

B: 至少在一月七日前到達紐約，十二日返回上海。

A: 我知道。我們有去紐約的直達航班。320 航班在一月六號上午八點從臺北起飛，當天晚上十點到達紐約。

B: 那麼回程票呢？

A: 回程是一月十二號上午八點從紐約起飛的 334 航班，第二天上午十點到達臺北。

B: 需要飛行多長時間。

A: 十八小時二十分種。

B: 天哪，要這麼長時間。請問票價多少？

A: 往返票價一共 35,600 元。

B: 好的。請幫我預訂這兩趟航班。

E. Role-play

Practise the following in English by using as many language skills learnt as

You are at the travel agent, giving and receiving the following information concerning flight reservation. Make a dialogue with your partner, you being the first to open the conversation.

Destination: _____

Departure date: _____

Number in party: _____

Special request: _____

Flight: _____

Return flight: _____

Price of he round-trip ticket: _____

Length of the flight: _____

Reference Answer:

A. Specialized Terms

Part 1

1.f   2.g   3.h   4.b   5.i   6.a   7.c   8.d

9.j   10.e

Part 2

1.g   2.b   3.h   4.j   5.i   6.l   7.a   8.e

9.d   10.c   11.f   12.k

D. Speaking Up

A: International Desk. How may I help you?

B: Yes, I'd like to check on flights from Taipei to New York.

A: When are you planning on traveling?

B: I need to be in New York by January 7th at the latest and return on the 12th.

A: I see. We have a direct flight to New York. You could leave Taipei on Flight 320 at 8:00 a.m. on January 6th, arriving in New York at 2:00 p.m. the same day.

B:　And what about the return?

A:　You'd leave New York on Flight 334 at 8:00 a.m. on January 12th, arriving in Taipei at 10:00 a.m. the following day.

B:　How long is the trip?

A:　Eighteen hours and twenty minutes.

B:　Oh, my! That's a long flight! And how much is it?

A:　The round-trip ticket is 35,600 NT dollars.

B:　OK, I think I'd like to go ahead and make a reservation.

Chapter 14

Reserving Post Conference Tours 會後旅遊預訂

Go over and expressions the following words.

encompass		v.	包含，包括
trails		n.	步道
tropical		a.	熱帶的
heritage		n.	遺產
Window of the World			世界之窗
all-in-one package			一攬子計畫，包價
gala night			盛大晚會
Bay Crossing Bridge			跨海大橋
compulsory		a.	必要的
insurance policy			保險單
insurance premium			保險費
excursion		n.	遠足旅遊
forward		v.	運送，轉交

Section 1
Interpretation Activities

A. Sentence Interpretation

1. First, find out the equivalents of the following words.

premiere	
in-depth consideration.	
spousal	
賞鳥散步	
恢復精神	

2. Read the following to your partner for him or her to put them down in Chinese or English.

1. Garden tours are one of the main events for the international conventions.

2. Convention Tours limited, Inc. is a premiere New York City tour operator and destination management company.

3. Tour is the one aspect of a convention that is most critical and deserves serious in-depth consideration.

4. If minimum numbers are not achieved, alternative arrangements or a complete refund of the published tour price will be made.

5. We create and manage distinctive city tours, evening entertainment programs, spousal and leisure time activities in connection with meetings and conferences held in the city.

6. 旅遊的價格不應該太高。雖然價格上會損失一點,但可以在旅遊登記報名上賺回可觀的收益。

7. 旅遊活動要在下午 4 點到 4 點半之前結束並返回旅館。這樣客人便有時間放鬆,恢復精神參加晚上的活動。

8. 與會者們忙碌地參加會議的期間,保證其家屬也有事做十分重要。

9. 第二天,安排了一次早晨賞鳥散步,你將有機會找出居住在弗雷澤島上的 354 種鳥類。

10. 如果您的旅遊需要與官方專案中列出的旅遊專案不同,請與會議經理們聯繫。

B. Passage Interpretation

1. First, find out the equivalents of the following words.

itinerary 營業額	

2. Read the following passages to yourself and render them into Chinese or English.

Passage 1

For those who want to extend their stay, we suggest one of the following options that will give an impression of New York City today. Please indicate your preference on the Registration Form. Please note that starting and finishing times as well as a full itinerary will be confirmed once the tour is booked.

Passage 2

會議旅遊已經成為國際旅遊業中非常重要的一部分。會議旅遊正在快速地以國際化的方式發展。僅在過去的十年時間裡就有 35,000 次會議活動,營業額達到 3.5 百萬歐元。歐洲,眾所周知的世界上最大的會議中心承辦了 60% 的全球性會議。

Reference Answers

A. Sentence Interpretation

1. words

premiere	首要的
in-depth consideration.	深層考慮
spousal	家屬
賞鳥散步	Bird Watching Walk
恢復精神	freshen up

2. sentences

1. 參觀花園是國際會議中一個主要的活動。

2. 會議旅遊有限公司是紐約市一家首要的旅遊經營與目的地管理公司。

3. 旅遊是會議活動中的最重要的一部分，同時也是需要認真地做深層考慮的一個方面。

4. 如果報名人數沒有滿，我們將做其他安排，或者按照公布的旅遊收費全額退還。

5. 結合在本市舉辦的會議和大會，我們公司開發管理與會議相關的獨具特色的都市旅遊，晚間娛樂活動以及家屬休閒活動。

6. Tour prices should not be too high. You can lose a small amount and make up the difference at registration.

7. Try to have tours back to the hotel by 4:00 to 4:30 pm. This will allow people to relax and freshen up for any evening

events.

8. While all the attendees are busy in the meetings, it's important to make sure the spouses stay busy too!

9. On the second day you will enjoy a morning Bird Watching Walk to seek out some of the 354 species of birds on Fraser Island.

10. If you require touring arrangements other than those offered in the official programme, please contact the meeting managers.

B. Passage Interpretation

1. words

itinerary	旅遊路線
營業額	turnover

2. paragraph

▌Passage 1

　　我們為那些希望延長逗留時間的客人提供以下幾種會後旅遊路線，客人可以從中挑選一條自己喜歡的路線。我們設計的每條路線都能夠讓您有機會了解現在的紐約。您只需在登記表中標明自己喜歡的路線即可。請您注意您一旦您做了預定，就意味著您確認了所選擇的旅遊項目的起始時間、結束時間以及整個路線。

Passage 2

Convention tourism has developed into an essential part of the international tourism industry. It is rapidly growing internationally with more than 35,000 convention events held in the last 10 years, with a turnover more than 3.5 billion euros. And Europe, known as the largest convention center in the world, hosts more than 60 percent of global conventions.

Section 2
Speaking Activities

A. Specialized Terms

Match the expressions on the left with the best Chinese equivalent on the right.

1. sightseeing and city tour _____A. 包價旅遊

2. shopping trip _____B. 導遊陪同旅遊

3. escorted tour _____C. 全天遊

4. package tour _____D. 水肺潛水

5. full-day excursion _____E. 名勝景點

6. cruise ship _____F. 城市觀光旅遊

7. the Bund _____G. 遊船

8. travel brochure 　　　　　　_____H. 旅遊資訊手冊

9. places of historic interests 　　_____I. 外灘

10. scuba-diving 　　　　　　　_____J. 購物旅遊

B. Sample Conversation

Read aloud.

Situation: Mr. Lee comes to Spring Travel Service to have a detailed talk about the post-conference tour of Taipei with Mr. Liu, clerk of the Spring Travel Service.

Mr. Liu:　Is there anything I can do for you?

Mr. Lee:　Yes. My friends told me Taipei is so wonderful a city. I want to see it with my own eyes. Can you suggest something?

Mr. Liu:　Many places in Taipei are worth seeing. Why not start with Chiang Kai-shek Memorial Hall?

Mr. Lee:　Then what?

Mr. Liu:　You may go to 228 Peace Park..

Mr. Lee:　I'm an architect. Are there any temple I can see around?

Mr. Liu:　Certainly. I suggest you going Longshan Temple.

Mr. Lee:　How can I get there?

Mr. Liu:　To save time, you can take a taxi.

Mr. Lee:　But I want a tour guide to escort me.

Mr. Liu:　In that case, a package tour will be fine with you.

Mr. Lee:　You're so thoughtful. Could you arrange this tour for me?

Mr. Liu: Yes, just a moment.

C. Functional Expressions

Read aloud and practice with your partner.

Could you tell me some places of historical interest in Taipei?
They are within easy access. The City Sightseeing Bus No.7
will take you there in succession. You may go out of the hotel, turn right, and you'll find the bus stop at the corner of the
street.

Lunch will at 12 o'clock at the Spring Restaurant near the
Lake.

Our guides are capable of both English and French, but bilingual service costs more.

We charge 1,200 NT dollars per person per day, excluding the
meals.

D. Speaking Up

**Translate the following sentences into English by using as
many language skills learnt as possible.**

1. ——_____?

    ——I'm very pleased to suggest that you go to the Lin Family
    Mansion and Garden and the S Longshan Temple.

    (用意：詢問旅遊景點)

2. ──Could you tell me how to go to these places?

___

_____.

(用意：介紹路線)

3. ──What about the meals?

___

_____.

(用意：介紹用餐安排)

4. 4. ──I want a tour guide to escort our group.

___

_____.

(用意：介紹導遊服務)

5. ──How much does the tour cost?

___

_____.

(用意：報價)

1. Could you tell me some places of historical interest in Taipei?

2. They are within easy access. The City Sightseeing Bus No. 7 will take you there in succession. You may go out of the hotel, turn right, and you'll find the bus stop at the corner of the street.

3. Lunch will at 12 o'clock at the Spring Restaurant near the Lake.

4. Our guides are capable of both English and French, but bilingual service costs more.

5. We charge 1,200 NT dollars person per day, excluding the meals.

E. Role-play

Practice the following in English according to the situations.

Situation 1

At the travel desk, a travel Reservationist reserves a one-day post-conference city tour of Taipei for Mr. Hilton, a meeting planner of a group of 28 members. The planner asks questions to find out necessary information. The clerk makes responses if necessary. You play the role of Mr. Hilton.

Your questions:

Which three places does a one day city tour include?

What can we expect to see in each of these places?

How long wills the tour last?

How much does the tour cost per person?

Can we hire a tour guide capable of speaking both English and French?

How much do you charge for the tour guide?

Situation 2

A: You are a clerk of Convention Tours Limited Inc. Your company is in charge of creating and managing the tour of the annual meeting of America Bankers Association. A potential guest calls for information about post convention tour registration. Please use the case given to answer the call.

B: You are an attendee of the annual meeting of America Bankers Association. You are calling to enquire about tour alternatives, price, and other details about the post convention tour.

Reference Answer

A. Specialized Terms

1.F　　2.J　　3.B　　4.A　　5.C　　6.G　　7.I　　8.H

9.E　　10.D

D. Speaking Up

1. Could you tell me some places of historical interest in Taipei?

2. They are within easy access. The City Sightseeing Bus No. 7 will take you there in succession. You may go out of the hotel, turn right, and you'll find the bus stop at the corner of the street.

3. Lunch will at 12 o'clock at the Spring Restaurant near the Lake.

4. Our guides are capable of both English and French, but bilingual service costs more.

5. We charge 1,200 NT dollars person per day, excluding the meals.

Chapter 15

Event Review Meetings 會後總結

Learn these words and expressions.

panel		n.	小組
barcode		n.	條碼
tentative		a.	嘗試的
outlet		n.	出口
protruding		a.	向外突出的
bump		v.	碰撞
simultaneous interpretation			同步口譯
acoustics		n.	聲學效果
make or break			顯著成功或徹底失敗
feedback		n.	回饋
promotional campaign			促銷活動

Section 1
Interpretation Activities

A. Sentence Interpretation

1. First, find out the equivalents of the following words.

session	
address	
會務費	

2. Read the following to your partner for him or her to put them down in Chinese or English.

1. When a convention program draws to a close, you will have the opportunity to review and assess the experience and satisfaction level of the convention event.

2. Sister Cities International and the Conference Planning Committee will consider your comments carefully when planning future events.

3. Please take a few moments to answer the following questions so we may improve upon future programs.

4. I also think a 3-day session would provide more time for the type of one on one interaction, as well as further small group discussions.

5. Although I agree with many of the positive overall comments about the Conference, I also believe there were some shortcomings that I would like to address.

6. 我認為會務費價格太高。

7. 有關此次會議的一些優缺點下面會詳細列出。希望這些在以後的行業會議中會有所改變。

8. 學習 2005 是一次非常成功的會議,但是由於行業的特點,仍然缺少了一些基本要素。

9. 請您用一點時間就此次分會提出任何其他的意見並對未來會議提出您的建議。

10. 當聽到每一位發言人的發言簡介幾乎雷同時,我真的感覺非常鬱悶。

B. Passage Interpretation

1. First, find out the equivalents of the following words.

回訪溝通函	

2. Read the following passages to yourself and render them into Chinese or English.

Passage 1

Thank you for completing the conference evaluations. We appreciate that you have taken the time to help the Global Health Council improve their Annual Conference. Your opinions, comments and suggestions are important to us. There are two different types of evaluations that can be completed. Option 1 is General Conference Evaluations and Option 2 is Specific Session Evaluation. You can do both of them or choose one. Thank you!

Passage 2

銷售發生在展覽結束後，所以你應該準備好一套回訪策略。寄發回訪溝通函，撥打回訪電話和銷售電話。展覽結束後還要實施銷售，三個月後要總結銷售成果。你將會吃驚地發現參加一次工業展示會受益良多。

Reference Answers

A. Sentence Interpretation

1. words

session	會期
address	強調，指出
會務費	conference admission fee

2. sentences

1. 會議接近尾聲時，你就有機會回顧與評估會議活動的經驗和滿意度。

2. 國際姐妹城市與會議策劃委員會策劃未來活動時會認真考慮您的意見。

3. 請您用幾分鐘時間回答下面幾個問題以便我們在未來活動中有所改進。

4. 我認為安排為期 3 天的分會可以提供更多一對一互動的時間，也可有更多時間展開小組討論。

5. 雖然我很同意許多就這次會議所做出的肯定評價，但我認為仍然存在一些缺點需要指出。

6. I think the price was rather high for the conference admission.

7. Some of the Good and bad points of the conference are detailed below. They are provided to encourage changes in all future industry conferences.

8. Learning 2005 was a very successful conference, but as is typical in our industry this conference still lacked some

fundamental elements.

a) Please take a moment to provide any additional comments about the session and suggestions for future meetings.

b) I was really getting frustrated when I heard that almost every speaker prefaces his presentation with essentially the same comments.

B. Passage Interpretation

1. words

回訪溝通函	follow-up communications

2. paragraph

▌Passage 1

　　謝謝您填寫會議評價表。我們感謝您抽出時間幫助世界健康委員會改進其年度會議。您的觀點及意見對我們十分重要。有兩種評估辦法可供您選擇。一種是會議總體評價，另一種是具體分會評價。您可選擇一種填寫，或者也可兩者均做。謝謝！

▌Passage 2

Sales are made after the show, so you should have a follow-up strategy in place! Send out follow-up communications, make follow-up phone and sales calls. Qualify sales post event and review the results in three months time - you'll be surprised how many will be attributed to your presence at a trade show.

Section 2
Speaking Activities

A. Specialized Terms

Match the expressions on the left with the best Chinese equivalent on the right.

Part 1

1. project manager   _____A. 籌備期

2. Expo-format   _____B. 框架展臺

3. capacity   _____C. 參展商

4. attendance   _____D. 專用洽談區

5. exhibitor   _____E. 反採購

6. professional visitor   _____F. 接待能力

7. lead time   _____G. 海外參展商

8. shell scheme   _____H. 專案經理

9. first-tier supplier   _____I. 參展人數

10. reversed on-site purchasing _____J. 專業觀眾

11. one-on-one meeting room _____K. 第一階供應商

12. overseas exhibitor 　　　　＿＿＿L. 展會形式

Part 2

1. dimmer 　　　　　　　A. 講壇，講臺

2. carousel projector 　　　B. 接線板

3. spotlight 　　　　　　　C. 遠端會議

4. roaming microphone 　　D. 寫字紙

5. teleprompter 　　　　　E. 幻燈機

6. flip chart 　　　　　　　F. 手持式麥克風

7. LCD panel 　　　　　　G. 聚光燈

8. easel 　　　　　　　　H. 液晶顯示幕

9. podium 　　　　　　　I. 三腳架

10. head receiver 　　　　J. 電視提詞器

11. house board 　　　　　K. 頭戴式耳機

12. teleconference 　　　　L. 燈光調節器

B. Sample Conversation

Read aloud.

Situation: Mr. Shelton, the convention service manager of Grand Hotel is hosting the evaluation meeting of the annual meeting of American Association of real estate. Mr. Smith, the meeting planner of the Association is presenting the meeting on behalf on the association.

CSM: Shall we start the evaluation meeting now, Mr. Smith?

MP: Is everyone who attended the pre-convention meeting here, Mr. Shelton?

CSM: Yes, Mr. Smith. All the directors are here. Catering director, F&B director, and the director of Security, Front Office Manager, Reservation Manager and our sales executive. They are all present.

MP: Well, let's start. First please allow me to give you all my heartfelt thanks. Your hard work and attentive service made our convention a great success. Our thanks especially go to the catering staff who provided our attendees with nice food of both western and Chinese styles.

CD: Thank you Mr. Smith. I'm very glad to hear that. It's our honor to serve you and our staff is looking forward to serving you again soon.

MP: I hope so. But I have to point out that two of our attendees complained the slow procedure of luggage delivery.

FOM: I'm sorry for it. But, Mr. Smith, you know yours is a big group. So it kept our bellman fairly busy to try to send the luggage to guests' room quickly enough. Unfortunately, we failed to notice that the two guests were rather tired. But we did try to make it up by offering them some refreshments on house.

MP: Thanks to your thoughtfulness and the two guests actually were deeply impressed by your attentive and friendly service later.

SE:　　We are so happy to know that all your attendees enjoyed their stay at our hotel. And we hope that we can have your next convention.

MP:　　It was just what I was thinking about, given your satisfactory security and reservation services. But I was wondering if you could low down the bill little. Our sponsor thinks that cost on equipment is still too high.

SE:　　But the equipment we provided with your convention is all brand-new most updated.

MP:　　I have to say that I can't agree more on this aspect. Your sound system did contribute a lot to the success of our convention. Beside this, I still think there is some room for lowing the bill down.

CSM:　　Then we can give you 30% discount if you let us do all your annual meetings.

MP:　　What about 50% if we give you all our annual meetings and seasonal meetings?

CSM:　　Thank you, Mr. Smith. We will try our best to make each of your meetings a great success.

C. Functional Expressions

Talking about similarities and differences

They had more exhibitors than those to be expected of ours.
Comparing all the previous Auto Expos, the biggest difference is size.

The Supertechnology Show is more expensive than Power Coating Europe.

There are four times as many exhibitors at CES as at Coating Europe.

Another difference is that these shows represent two separate markets for us.

The main similarity is that many of the big name companies will be exhibiting at both Expos.

What the buyer will achieve will equal to that at 30 traditional exhibitions.

Talking about advantages and disadvantages

Would it be more appropriate to ...

The only drawback is ...

How is ...going for you?

Comparing the two shows, ...

You're absolutely right, but the problem is ...

The main advantage of ... is ...

D. Speaking Up

1. 參加本屆展會的參展商人數是去年的四倍。

2. 本應該為採購參展商事先安排與供應商一對一的洽談。

3. 參加本次展覽的一大好處是我們見到了來自世界各地的零售商。

4. 但是另一方面，我們應該多提供一些場地。

5. 展會唯一的不足是成本太高了。

E. Role-play

Practice the conversation in English according to the situation.

　　You are Mr. William Thompson, the meeting planner of the Global Education council. You are presenting the post convention meeting summarizing the good and bad points of the 45th annual conference of the council that was headquartered at Holiday Inn Tibet.

Reference Answer

A. Specialized Terms

Part 1

1.H　　2.L　　3.F　　4.I　　5.C　　6.J　　7.A　　8.B
9.K　　10.E　　11.D　　12.G

Part 2

1.L　　2.E　　3.G　　4.F　　5.J　　6.D　　7.H　　8.I
9.A　　10.K　　11.B　　12.C

D. Speaking Up

1. There are four times as many exhibitors at the expo as last time.

2. Sourcing exhibitors should have been prearranged for one-on-one meetings with suppliers.

3. One big advantage of attending this exhibiting is that we have met retailers from all over the country.

4. But on the other hand, we could have offered larger exhibition area.

5. The only drawback of this expo is the cost.

官網

國家圖書館出版品預行編目資料

上班天天說英語，輕鬆駕馭國際會議：擴大詞彙、增進口說能力、加強翻譯，實用會展英語一網打盡！ / 吳雲 主編 . -- 第一版 . -- 臺北市：崧燁文化事業有限公司 , 2023.03
面；　公分
POD 版
ISBN 978-626-357-140-2(平裝)
1.CST: 英語 2.CST: 會議 3.CST: 讀本
805.188 112000574

上班天天說英語，輕鬆駕馭國際會議：擴大詞彙、增進口說能力、加強翻譯，實用會展英語一網打盡！

臉書

主　　　編：吳雲
發 行 人：黃振庭
出 版 者：崧燁文化事業有限公司
發 行 者：崧燁文化事業有限公司
E - m a i l：sonbookservice@gmail.com
粉 絲 頁：https://www.facebook.com/sonbookss/
網　　　址：https://sonbook.net/
地　　　址：臺北市中正區重慶南路一段六十一號八樓 815 室
Rm. 815, 8F., No.61, Sec. 1, Chongqing S. Rd., Zhongzheng Dist., Taipei City 100, Taiwan
電　　　話：(02)2370-3310　　傳　　　真：(02) 2388-1990
印　　　刷：京峯彩色印刷有限公司（京峰數位）
律師顧問：廣華律師事務所 張珮琦律師

定　　　價：350 元
發行日期：2023 年 03 月第一版
◎本書以 POD 印製